GUNS AND ATTITUDE

GUNS AND ATTITUDE

PAIN AND AGONY™ BOOK THREE

MICHAEL ANDERLE

This book is a work of fiction. All of the characters, organizations, and events portrayed in this novel are either products of the author's imagination or are used fictitiously. Sometimes both.

Copyright © 2021 LMBPN Publishing
Cover Art by Jake @ J Caleb Design
http://jcalebdesign.com / jcalebdesign@gmail.com
Cover copyright © LMBPN Publishing
A Michael Anderle Production

LMBPN Publishing supports the right to free expression and the value of copyright. The purpose of copyright is to encourage writers and artists to produce the creative works that enrich our culture.

The distribution of this book without permission is a theft of the author's intellectual property. If you would like permission to use material from the book (other than for review purposes), please contact support@lmbpn.com. Thank you for your support of the author's rights.

LMBPN Publishing
PMB 196, 2540 South Maryland Pkwy
Las Vegas, NV 89109

Version 1.00, November 2021
ebook ISBN: 978-1-68500-528-3
Print ISBN: 978-1-68500-529-0

THE GUNS AND ATTITUDE TEAM

Thanks to the Beta Readers
Larry Omans, Kelly O'Donnell, Rachel Beckford, John Ashmore

Thanks to the JIT Readers

Dave Hicks
Dorothy Lloyd
Zacc Pelter
Peter Manis
Diane L. Smith
Deb Mader
Jeff Goode
Angel LaVey

If I've missed anyone, please let me know!

Editor
The Skyhunter Editing Team

DEDICATION

*To Family, Friends and
Those Who Love
to Read.
May We All Enjoy Grace
to Live the Life We Are
Called.*

— Michael

CHAPTER ONE

Pain and Agony had gone with the decision to procure magnetic signs for the outside of Bertha. These would add authenticity to whatever business they used as a bluff on any given day to try to gain access to various places during an investigation. The signs all began with *P & A* but the *Flower Delivery, Caterers, Wedding Planners, Plumbing,* and *Electrical*, along with half a dozen others, were changed as needed.

With their landlady Ahjoomenoni's seed money from a job they had completed to her satisfaction a month earlier, the partners had rented office space. After a careful search for the right premises, they chose one on the second floor in an older but well-kept two-story building not very far from the city center.

The location had several things in its favor. It wasn't in one of the ubiquitous office complexes in the suburbs just outside the city where all buildings were almost identical in their banality. A side lot provided more than enough parking. The building held eight offices on the second floor, four on each side of the hallway into which the elevator, located at the end of the entrance hallway, opened.

A flight of stairs near the front was available if someone was in more of a hurry and didn't want to take the time to trudge down the hallway to the elevator. The partners usually used the stairs and often two at a time. They saw it as a chance to squeeze some exercise in.

Their office was the first one on the left coming up the stairs and the last on the right if one chose the elevator.

As far as they were concerned, though, one of the building's best features was that the first floor only accommodated six offices. It could have held eight, but the two spaces that fronted the sidewalk were occupied by a family that believed in food service.

The building had one door in the middle that led to the offices inside. Each of the dining establishments had separate entrances that opened directly onto the sidewalk.

On the south side of the center door was Pasha's's Deli that was open from 6:00 am until 3:00 pm to serve the breakfast and lunch hour crowds. They served bagels—you name it, they had it —sandwiches fully-stacked, French fried potatoes only, soups that changed daily, and some damn fine coffee.

The establishment on the north side of the entrance that led to the offices inside was occupied by Masha's Deli. It was open from 9:00 pm until 5:00 am and served foods that a breakfast diner with a grill would typically offer—any style eggs, toast from plain to French, sausages, be it links or patties, hash-browned or cubed potatoes, and of course, some damn fine coffee.

The women who ran the two delis were identical twins. Pasha, which in Hebrew meant Daughter of God, and Masha, Rebellious woman in Hebrew. Twins they were born, twins they would live, and twins they would die. One of their strongest bonds was a shared sense of humor. Another was the belief that dinner was a time when families should gather at home, which is why neither of their delis was open during the dinner hour. One thing they didn't share was internal body clocks. Pasha had always been an early riser. Masha had always been hard to get out of bed before noon.

They had subjected their parents to more than a few trials while they were being raised. After they had both finished college, they made a joint decision and convinced their parents that providing food was a noble and necessary occupation.

Rather than making things overly complicated by trying to open a twenty-four-hour restaurant that catered to everyone, they split the difference and opened two small, almost side-by-side delis, both of which encouraged people to go home to enjoy family dinnertime.

For Pain and Agony, who didn't keep what anyone would consider regular hours, the twins were a godsend.

What wasn't quite a godsend was their first hire. All Yolanda had to do between her incessant gum-snapping while she manned the desk in their small reception area was answer the phone, transfer a call if one of her bosses was in, or take a legible memo if they were both out.

While there was a little filing here and there, it wasn't much. They hadn't been in business long enough for the paperwork to have piled up.

The partners had just returned from an annoying morning spent sifting through the public records at the city clerk's office downtown, where they had to fill out an individual form for each record they wanted to look at. The clerk, whose desk plate read Joan Reedy, refused to pull more than one file at a time.

Technically speaking, that was well within her designated obligations. The reasoning behind the city's one file at a time policy was to make sure there was enough work for the number of employees the city clerk's record office insisted were necessary. If one clerk could pull more than one record at a time, it would be hard to justify the number of staff that was needed. If one clerk could, heaven forbid, pull eight files at once, the number of man-hours would take a drastic cut, and no one on Joan Reedy's side of the desk wanted that.

It didn't matter that Pain and Agony had requested eight files, all of them consecutively numbered. The woman would only pull one at a time. They would then pay to have copies made, return the file, and wait for Lazy-bones-Joan to meander through the stacks to pull the next one.

"Maybe," Pain suggested as they finally left the record clerk's office, "we should train Yolanda to handle simple tasks like this."

"I don't know, partner," she responded as they enjoyed the sunshine on their four-block walk to the office. "That would require her to be able to walk and chew gum at the same time."

With nothing pressing on their schedule, they were trying to do a little follow-up research on a job they had finished two weeks after they had their office squared away and brought in a receptionist from a temp company creatively named Hire-A-Temp.

It had been an ugly job from all perspectives, but the successful completion had made it feel worthwhile. A particular name, though, had caught their attention. It was prominent enough to send them to the records clerk's office in an effort to clear up a few questions.

"Do you think," Pain asked as they stopped at a street vendor's falafel stand, "that we'll ever have a missing person's case that requires us to simply trace a missing person and not a terrorist plot or, as in this latest one, a human trafficking ring?"

"That would be a nice change of pace," Agony agreed and asked for some extra hummus. They sat on a bench and enjoyed their lunch. It was a pleasant interlude during which to disengage their minds from their experience with Joan the Moan before they returned to their office and the gum-snapping receptionist.

She tapped the shoulder bag she used to hold the files they had copied which now rested on the bench between them.

"That is a scary name, Pain."

"A very scary name," he agreed as he took a bite of his falafel, appreciative of having something other than a hot dog or a taco available from a street cart. "Let's hope we're wrong."

"And if we aren't?" It was something they had to consider, but she asked the question reluctantly.

"Does the word 'blowback' mean anything to you?"

"My thoughts exactly. Damn, this is the best hummus in the city."

Pain finished his lunch and leaned back. "We fucked with a human trafficking ring that probably pulled in a hundred-K a day, and that's if they were only a local organization. We may never know the full extent of their connections."

The pleasant lunch finished, they completed the walk to the office and up the stairs.

"So I said, like, no." Yolanda was on her cell, much too conscientious an employee to tie up her employers' phone line in case a call came through. "I mean, 'look how big my wide-screen is,' is no more impressive than 'listen to how loud my muffler is.' What the hell do either of those have to do with how big his—whoops, gotta go."

"Hi, bosses," their receptionist managed to say before she went to work torturing her gum again. "Did you find what you were looking for?"

Shit, Agony thought. *If gum-smacking was an Olympic event, this girl would be at least a bronze medalist.*

"Are there any messages?" she asked the girl as they strolled in and were about to head to her office. It was a good time to sort through their patience-stretching, Xerox-copied, old but not yet dust-covered files and try to make some sense of them.

"Only some guy from the FBI wondering if you two were both in. He said something about needing to serve some warrants or something."

"The FBI called?" Both the partners' antennas were immediately up but Pain was the first one to speak.

"Uh-huh." Yolanda nodded vigorously.

"And he wanted to make sure we were both in because he wanted to serve us a warrant?" He narrowed his eyes.

"Yeah. It sounded real official and everything."

"Take yourself to Pasha's." He pulled his wallet out and handed her a ten-dollar bill. "And enjoy lunch on us."

"Seriously?"

"Seriously." He pointed her toward the door. "Go."

"You guys are great bosses."

"Yeah," he agreed, "we're the best."

"Does the FBI usually call in advance to serve a warrant?" Agony asked as their receptionist stepped through the door.

"Your daily allotment of stupid questions has been reached," he responded bluntly.

"Impersonating the Feds? How pissy are these pricks?"

"Hey, we're talking about impersonating a government agent!" Pain was in danger of exploding into a rant. "Does that take any great talent? How often have you heard me say that Uncle Sam usually gets the lowest sludge from the bottom of the barrel? Because if they were as smart as they were unscrupulous—"

"I know." She quoted the Gospel according to Pain. "They'd work for the government. Remind me again about your former employer?"

"What can I say?" He shrugged. "I needed the money."

Yolanda needed the money too, but not enough to have been intercepted halfway down the stairs and forced into the office as a human shield. Almost a dozen men in suits burst through the door and the leader shouted, "FBI! Everyone down on the floor!"

"You heard the man, Yolanda!" Pain commanded. "Get down on the floor and find a corner."

The girl used the lesson every school kid had learned during fire drills. She stopped, dropped, and rolled until she curled in a corner.

He grabbed a stack of copy paper from the desk and tossed it toward the FBI impersonators. The scattered paper floated slowly downward and blocked everyone's vision for anything resembling a clean shot at a clear target. That didn't stop the attackers from trying, however, and they opened fire with real enthusiasm. The air in the room looked like a wintery snow-globe minus the quaint village or Santa's workshop.

"I'll go in high and come back low," Pain informed Agony quickly after they'd spun around the corner that led to their offices. "Aim to wound and not to kill."

"No killing?" She sounded disappointed.

"Yes to blood and ballistics." He was adamant. "No to dead bodies. There is way too much paperwork involved."

She knew he was wearing his full Wonderboy-Underoos—or Wonderoos as she had taken to calling his custom-made body-hugging protective suit. As long as he could avoid a headshot, he'd be fine. She snatched up her faithful S & W, held it out and around the corner, and fired a couple of high warning shots to give him a second or two of cover.

He used the time wisely, vaulted onto Yolanda's desk, and launched himself as a horizontal missile at the uninvited guests. Six of them were knocked flat on their backs. A six-foot-four, two-hundred-and-forty-pound body that stretched almost ten-foot from fingers to toes could do that.

Agony spun around the corner and fired four more shots aimed at anything below the kneecaps. Four quick screams followed, none of them Pain's, to confirm that all the bullets had found a target.

A sawed-off shotgun careened toward her, a gift from her partner, and she cocked it as he shouted, "Aim higher this time!" and launched himself from behind the gang. He stayed as close to the floor as he could and swept a large number of legs out from under their assailants as he rolled through them.

The blast from her newly acquired shotgun made contact

with several arms and shoulders and maybe even a face or two. It was filled with buckshot, so unless it was fired directly into a face from four feet or closer, no serious harm would be done.

Pain, still tangled on the floor with the bodies he'd upended, scooped up every weapon the faux-FBI agents had dropped and slid all of them to his partner.

"Oh," she said loudly enough for everyone to hear, "I like this one!" She let loose with a five-second blast from an RJ-sub, all above head level as per her partner's request.

When the sound subsided, she shouted and counted down quickly. "Next burst in five! Four! Three! Two! One!"

Pain, still entangled with bodies, had to cover his head to protect it from the shoes and boots and…one pair of sandals with white socks? He thought he caught a fleeting glimpse of those as the mad scramble to escape began.

In moments, the would-be assassins managed to run, limp, and drag their wounded colleagues out the door. While some rushed to the elevator as a group endeavor, the more ambulatory among them took the stairs.

The elevator doors opened and Harry and Harriet Elliot, a sweet older couple who had come for their weekly adjustment by their chiropractor, saw the crowd waiting in the hall and stepped out of their way as quickly as possible.

"Don't worry, honey." Harry patted his wife's shoulder as the group rushed in and the crowded elevator made its way downward. "I saw some blood. They were probably part of one of those group-counseling sessions the new psychologist in suite 2-E likes to hold."

"His sessions do sometimes get a little loud," she agreed and took the hand of her husband of forty years. "Now let's go see what kind of magic Dr. Carville can do with our old decrepit bones today."

"I am all in favor of that." He smiled. "As long as he doesn't try to adjust any bones in that pretty face of yours."

They had enjoyed forty years of marital bliss, not to mention the prior ten years when they'd shacked up together before they gave in to their parents' wish to make it official and finally give them some grandchildren. Even after all that time, the only thing Harry Elliot saw in his wife's face was the young woman he'd fallen in love with so many decades before.

They continued to Dr. Carville's office in suite 3-D. He made sure he had his little blue pill ready to wash down as soon as their sessions were over. The doctor and his staff would do their weekly magic with their old bones. The little blue pill would do the rest once they got home.

"Can I come out now?" Yolanda gasped in her corner. It was hard for her to get the words out since she had swallowed her gum during the excitement and it was still stuck in her throat.

Pain helped her up and began to brush debris from her head. Agony took a bottle of water from the mini-fridge and offered it to her to help wash down both the gum and the dust as they teamed up to guide the temp to her receptionist's chair.

"Thank you." The girl sat, gulped a little of the water, and began to gather her belongings. "Please don't give me a bad review." She looked at each of her employers in turn. "But dodging flying bullets and stuff was not mentioned when they assigned me here."

She stood and the partners made sure her legs weren't too wobbly to walk as they guided her out the door and suggested the elevator as opposed to the stairs.

"We'll give you nothing but a five-star review, Yolanda," Agony assured her. "And we'll let your supervisors at Hire-A-Temp know that it was my partner and I who decided to close down for a few weeks. We will contact them again when we reopen for business and need a new hire."

"Thanks." Yolanda sounded sincere as she dug out another stick of gum from her purse and went to work on it. "But you might also wanna work on a more detailed description of the job requirements."

"Thank you for the advice." She couldn't argue with a thing their gum-smacking former receptionist said. "We'll work on that."

They watched as she made it safely down the hallway and stepped into an empty elevator.

"I don't think I'd want to work for us either," Pain had to admit as he and his partner turned to their office, intending to survey the damage. He closed the door and they both paused as the tinkle of falling glass punctuated the action.

"Aw, man." Agony was the first to realize what the sound meant. "I've never had an office door with a window of etched glass before."

"It was a first for both of us." Pain's voice showed that he shared her sorrow.

Most doors were simply doors, but this one had been special-ordered and had only been installed four days earlier. The frame was an attractive mahogany, with an etched glass window fitted into the upper half that read, *P & A Investigations*. It had been a thing of beauty and one of their few splurges.

With her past as a cop and his past as a servant of Uncle Sam —neither of which ended with anything resembling an award for Meritorious Services through no fault of their own—the etched glass was symbolic. It meant that they were ready to pursue justice on terms they could both be proud of. They would no longer have to worry about having to answer to power-hungry bosses cutting back-room deals and feeding them and their former, now-dead partners to the wolves.

Agony had Alex and Pain had Kip, and both of them had a plethora of unanswered questions that the higher-ups had squashed the second any query had been raised.

"You have to be shittin' me," a man said behind them as they started to pick up the pieces of what was left of the window. "I've got fourteen offices to clean tonight during one eight-hour shift. How many of those hours am I gonna hafta spend cleaning up the first one?"

"None, Zeke." Pain looked up and addressed the one-man evening custodial staff who had probably pushed his cart onto the elevator when it had opened on the first floor and Yolanda kissed the building goodbye.

Zeke, being the occupant of a body that had survived more than sixty circles around the sun, shook his head.

"Will you two amateurs please stand up and get out of my way so I can do my job?"

CHAPTER TWO

The partners stood to allow the man to go about his business. During the brief time they'd occupied their new office and due to the hours they kept, they had run into the one-man janitorial staff at the end of more than one long day.

When he was younger, the still trim custodian could have matched the ex-agent in height, inch for inch, but age had taken its toll. If the three of them stood upright side by side, Zeke still had at least three inches on Agony but had lost the battle to her partner.

"Tell us what you need...Deke," Pain told him, "and we'll do our best to get you back on track."

"His name is Zeke." Agony corrected her partner hastily. At least she remembered that much from the late-night hours when they had run into him and was surprised that her partner had the custodian's name wrong.

"Zeke," he agreed, "to his family and friends, but Deke to his fans and to us kids who were too tall for their shoes and tried to duplicate his moves on the playground."

"So." The custodian straightened and asked, "Are you looking for an autograph from an old fossil?"

"No." Pain picked up a sheet of copy paper from the floor, crumpled it, and tossed it to the custodian. "Get a shot past me and through what's left of the door's window."

"Shit, sonny." The janitor caught the crumpled sheet. "The window's too easy. What about the little wastebasket in the corner?" He gestured to the corner of the office where Yolanda had somehow managed to not move the small circular wastebasket when she ducked from the bullets.

"Go ahead and try," the ex-agent challenged him.

"Hhmm," Zeke mumbled loudly enough for Agony to hear, "big and dumb as they come."

Zeke deked left and then right, got his opponent off his feet with his arms spread wide, and tossed an underhanded bankshot at the wall that ended up in the wastebasket, hitting nothing but net.

Having been properly schooled, Pain turned to his partner. "May I introduce you to Zeke the Deke, the man who had more moves on the court than should have been legal until he blew his Achilles' during his second season of pro ball." He proffered his hand. "It's an honor to meet you."

"The pleasure is all yours." Zeke was gracious enough to shake his hand. "And before you ask, the tendon is fine. It's my knees that give me hell these days."

"How about we help you out a little?" Pain offered. It wasn't as if they weren't used to cleaning up after themselves.

He retrieved a broom and a dustpan as Agony brought three bottles of beer from the fridge, popped their caps, and passed them around. She went to work emptying the wastebaskets. The beer was cold and a fine example of a micro-brew.

The janitor decided to take Yolanda's seat and direct the action. Maybe this wouldn't be such a bad shift after all. Unfortunately, those happy thoughts disappeared when footsteps pounded up the stairs and the boys in blue rushed in.

"What do you want to bet," Pain muttered as he laid his broom on the floor, "that they're not here to help us tidy up?"

Agony sank to her knees and laced her finders together on top of her head and in plain sight. "Maybe we can talk them into at least gathering some brass and running a few ballistic tests."

"I won't hold my breath." Pain settled onto his knees and laced his hands as he advised the custodian, "Zeke? You might want to join us."

"What the hell is going on now?" The man felt he had the right to ask.

"If you don't want to become collateral damage," Agony advised, "you might want to join us down here—now!"

"Oh, sweet baby of Mary and Joseph." Zeke took one last quick sip of the brew and assumed the position.

"Down! Down! Everybody down!" the first officer up the stairs shouted as he entered the office, followed by half a dozen more boys in blue.

"Already done, officer." Pain stated the obvious. "Skip to the next part."

"We had calls reporting gunfire." The sarcasm flew right past the officer's head. "A lot of calls and a lot of gunfire."

"Take a look around," Agony added, "and you tell us if the reports were accurate or not."

"Whose office is this?" The last man up the stairs wore a suit as opposed to a uniform.

"This is the office of P & A Investigations," Pain answered. "If the window to our door hadn't been shot to hell it would clearly state that...Officer?"

"Detective." The trim man corrected him wearily. "Detective Bontail. And you are?"

"I'm the *P*," Pain answered and nodded toward his partner. "She's the *A*."

"And who is he?" Detective Bontail pointed at the third

kneeling civilian who seemed to be trying to shift his weight constantly from one knee to the other.

"He," Zeke answered for himself, "is an old man trying to do his job."

"Which is?"

"A jazz pianist. With one quick push of a button, my cart full of mops and buckets turns into a baby grand. I was here to audition for a wedding reception gig."

"Weapons?" the detective asked.

"I have a few of them stacked there near the hallway." Agony nodded to where she had left the ones Pain had tossed to her and added, "None of them ours."

"All right." Detective Bontail had heard enough to believe that the threat level was now low and signaled to his men to holster their guns. "Let's see if we can make some sense out of this." He started to hand out assignments but was interrupted by another group, this one dressed in FBI-approved bland, dark suits.

"We'll take it from here," a stern voice announced.

"And who the hell is we?" The detective turned, not at all happy and ready to draw his weapon.

"FBI." The man held out an official badge for all to see. "Special Agent Marshal Buchanan. Both the scene and investigation are now under federal jurisdiction."

"By whose authorization, Agent Buchanan?" Detective Bontail had seldom won a pissing contest with the feds but that didn't mean he wasn't willing to get into another one.

"*Special* Agent Buchanan." The Fed faced him squarely. "Officer..."

"*Detective* Bontail, or did me wearing a suit instead of a uniform confuse you?"

"Officer, detective, or chief of police." Buchanan sneered. "It doesn't matter. I'm telling you that you are about to wade waist-deep into a federal investigation you want no part of."

"The only thing I'm wading in is a river of federal shit."

"Is it always like this with you two?" Zeke asked quietly. The three of them remained kneeling with their hands still on their heads.

"Yes." The partners nodded and answered in unison but kept their voices down.

"But only on slow days," Pain added. "You should see us during our busy season."

"I think I'll take a pass on that." The janitor shook his head. "I'm too old for this shit and my knees are way too old and ragged for me to rest on them this long."

"You won't quit on us, will you, Zeke?" Agony felt the guilt settle in.

"Not only quit on you." Zeke made no effort to assuage her guilt and simply stated the truth. "Quit on this whole building. You have no idea how messy those other offices can get."

"I can only imagine," Pain sympathized, "but you never have to walk in until after they've left their messes behind. This mess is a little more personal, isn't it?"

"My knees would certainly agree with that," Zeke the Deke replied, the baller the sports reporters used to call The Man with a Thousand Moves and who now wondered how many moves it would take him to get back to a standing position.

The Detective Bontail and Special Agent Marshal Buchanan pissing match had reached the shouting stage. Both their squads watched and started taking bets as to which way the match would go. The smart money was on the feds. Between the shouting, they both made phone calls and tried to get through to their department heads.

Pain managed to get the attention of a lower-ranking fed, pointed at the old custodian, and motioned that they would try to get him into a more comfortable position. The agent nodded.

Moving slowly so as to not draw any additional attention, the partners helped Zeke to sit so he could rest his back against a wall and stretch his legs out while he massaged his aching joints.

They had also maneuvered themselves into the same position but with Agony seated next to the old man and Pain on her other side. This way, they were better able to whisper together as they watched and listened to the drama unfolding between the two combatants squared off in the middle of the room.

"I knew I should have brought some popcorn," was Pain's first quiet observation.

"It probably wouldn't have been worth the trouble." She was quickly becoming bored. "We've both seen this movie before and we know who wins. There isn't much suspense."

"But this time," he pointed out, "we want the mean old feds to win."

"Whatever for?" She wanted to hear his reasoning.

"You've already met some of my former home team—" he managed to say before she cut him off.

"None of whom I have been impressed with enough to put on a cheerleader's outfit and go all rah-rah for as I waved my pom-poms."

"I understand." And he did. His fellow feds had not exactly represented themselves in anything that could be considered an endearing manner. "But all they have done is tried to intimidate. What we need to keep in mind is the fact that someone on your team in blue has put a hit out on you, and we don't know if that is still active or not. Do you want to be taken into their custody and left vulnerable for long enough for someone to finish the job?"

That jab of wisdom hit her hard and fast and she realized that even though no further attempts had been made on her life, it didn't mean the contract had expired.

"Rah-rah-zis-boom-bah-gooooo feds!" She chanted her quiet cheer as the jurisdictional battle continued to rage between the leaders of Team Blue and Team Dark Suit & Tie.

"Maybe it's time to help to tip the game," Pain suggested.

"If you wanna tip the game..." Zeke the Deke interjected himself into the conversation. "Tip the ball. They'll follow wherever it bounces and lose the big-picture focus. But don't tip the points of the guns in my direction."

"Deal," the ex-agent assured him. "Stay low."

"It's gonna be hard for me to go high without some assistance," the man answered. "Even my ass is sore now."

There was a slight pause in the shouting match between the two head honchos and Pain took full advantage of it.

"Excuse me!" he called from his position on the floor. "Officer Montail and Agent Buchanan."

"*Detective* Bontail!" The captain of Team Blue spun and corrected him.

"*Special* Agent Buchanan!" The leader of the Men in Drab also spun.

He had succeeded in his effort to provide the two with a common enemy long enough for them to be able to set aside their petty jurisdictional squabble for a moment.

"We might be able to help you two children resolve this."

"And how might you be able to do that?" Special Agent Marshal Buchanan already knew he would eventually win the battle with the cop-squad detective but was tired of waiting on hold for his director to pick up the damn phone.

"What he said." Detective Bontail was also tired of waiting for an answer as his call was constantly rerouted higher up the food chain.

"We have a file"—Pain used his gentle but firm voice—"that will probably help clarify the situation here."

"You have a file," the fed mocked. "Now I am truly impressed."

"Where is the file?" the detective sounded a little more willing to hear him out.

"I'll show you but first, someone has to help our friend here with the bad knees onto his chair—the one he was sitting in before everyone busted in. If not, continue with your shouting and waiting for one of your parents to answer the phone. Of course, they'll tell you to play nice with each other before your other playmates get bored with their staring and glaring at each other contests and start to wander off."

"Help the old man up." The detective took the lead since his boys had been the first to arrive at the scene.

Two officers assisted Zeke off the floor and into the chair at Yolanda's desk. Once seated, the custodian didn't waste any time. He took hold of the bottle of now room-temperature microbrew and downed the remainder in one long and satisfying gulp.

"You were saying?" Special Agent Buchanan prodded.

"There is a folder on the floor in the hallway leading to the offices." At least that was where he thought his partner had tossed it when the original intruders had burst in and opened fire. The four aggravating hours they'd spent at the city's records clerk's office earlier that day might prove to not be wasted after all.

No one waited for any other explanation. A minor fed and a sergeant in blue found and fought over the file and played a tug of war with it to determine who could prevail at presenting it to their bosses.

"Put the damn thing down on the desk!" Pain shouted. "Skim through it at the same time and you'll both recognize the name."

The tug of war ended and the file was laid open. Zeke had a front-row seat as the fed's and the detective's eyes widened when they scanned through it and recognized the name.

"It's all yours, Agent Buchanan." Detective Bontail grinned at his adversary and stepped back. "Come on, troops. This one has feds written all over it."

The detective and his squad made a quick, orderly exit.

"That's *Special* Agent Buchanan!" His parting shot sounded a little desperate.

"Maybe you're special to your mother," the detective retorted, "but you're nothing but a suit-wearing pile of shit to the rest of us."

Having seen the name in the file, Detective Bontail was glad to have lost that battle.

Special Agent Buchanan could understand why the cops were suddenly glad to hand this to them.

"We will stand now," Agony informed him. She preferred to hold conversations with someone at eye level instead of having to look up at them from the floor.

The partners rose in unison.

"Questions?" Pain asked.

"A long list of questions," the agent answered, "but none that I intend to ask here. We'll all take a ride now.

"Shit." Zeke rose. "I still got thirteen offices left to clean."

"And one of my men will accompany you," the agent informed him. "But you are done with this one for the night."

"Thank God for small favors," the janitor muttered as he took hold of his cart and headed to office 2-B. He was followed by an agent whose job it was to make sure he didn't suddenly sneak back into the office to retrieve something behind their backs.

Once in the hallway, the agents sealed the door with their black-and-white FBI crime-scene tape and the partners were quickly cuffed, their hands behind their backs.

"Seriously?" Pain asked as he complied peacefully with the restraints. "Are we under arrest now?"

"Arrest is such a harsh term," Buchanan answered. "Let's say these are for your safety. We don't want either of you to do anything stupid that might lead to further complications."

"Can we at least grab a quick order to go from Masha's?" he asked as they were marched down the stairs.

"What? You don't like fed food?"

"I'm not craving stale cheese-filled crackers and moldy Mr. Peanut bars from vending machines right now."

"Well then," the man informed him, "you might have to go hungry tonight."

With that, they were led to and thrust into separate black sedans—Federal Interrogation Techniques 101: Keep the suspects separated.

CHAPTER THREE

No one asked them any questions during the drive to wherever their destination was and both of them hoped they were at least headed to the same building. No questions were answered either. Special Agent Marshal Buchanan had no Chatty-Cathy's among his crew.

Even though handcuffed, they at least hadn't had hoods thrown over their heads so they could watch as the three-car cavalcade wound into a parking garage under the FBI's field office just inside the city limits.

They were escorted out of the vehicles and toward the elevators where the agents made no effort at geniality while they waited for the doors to open.

"Another parking garage." Pain aimed his comment at his partner.

"And another group of your friends," she responded tartly. "Remind me again how often good things happen in parking garages."

The doors opened, and with the elevator not being large enough to carry the whole entourage at once, Pain's team entered first. An agent pressed the button and the doors closed. Buchanan remained behind in her group.

"Your partner has quite an interesting history." He leaned close enough for her to get a whiff of his cologne. Not only was it an unfortunate choice of fragrance, but she realized that he probably reapplied it several times each day. The build-up of the applications left him reeking after a twelve-hour day, but she decided to try to breathe through her mouth and not her nose. This was not the most opportune time to give the man any grooming tips.

"Yes," she answered, "he does."

"As do you."

The tone in his voice sent a quick chill down her spine and she chose silence as her response.

The elevator dinged again and they all squeezed in together.

Breathe through your mouth, she reminded herself, *and pray for a lower floor destination.*

To her relief, it was only a three-floor ride. When the doors opened, she was the first to step off and drew a quick breath of stale but at least not cologne-filled air. She was escorted down the hallway and to her even greater relief, was led into an interrogation room where her partner sat behind a good-sized rectangular table, his hands no longer cuffed.

"Welcome to Spook Central." He greeted her cheerfully.

"Charming digs," she replied as her hands were un-cuffed and she was directed to a seat on his side of the table.

"Maybe we should have taken our chances with my team," she griped as she sat.

"It's too early to tell. Did you learn anything?"

"Yeah. Eau-de-agent-cologne can be classified as cruel and unusual punishment in a confined space."

"Is that where that smell was coming from back in the office? There were too many occupants for me to narrow it down."

"Trust me," she answered as she searched the table for a box of tissues that she could pull one out of and scrunch a few pieces up to jam into her nostrils. "I shared an elevator with him. Do you think they'll provide us with oxygen masks?"

"It's probably not high on their agenda." He sighed. "Maybe the cologne is a strategic choice used for the purposes of getting faster confessions."

"Okay..." She nodded, "I can see that but how do you explain the haircut? It's a strange one, especially for a fed."

"Some things defy explanations."

Their conversation came to an abrupt end when the agent in question strode into the room, dismissed the others, took a seat across from them, and put a file folder down in front of him.

He flipped through it, *tsk-tsking* all the way.

Never be the first one to speak. Never answer a question before it is asked. Never think for a moment that the one on the other side of the table has your best interests in mind.

Pain and Agony had spent enough time on the other side of the table that they could have written a manual on how to behave while being interrogated.

As Special Agent Marshal Buchanan perused the file, they occupied their time by trying to decide what particular look the agent had tried to achieve with his choice of hair design. It was almost a brush-cut on the sides and back, but a top of dark hair was combed forward and lightly greased with a curling-back wave at the front to keep his forehead clear.

If he was freshly out of a shower, the front wave would probably have been long enough to reach his eyes. It looked like a cross between punk, Mohawk, and pompadour—not a particularly complimentary look but these days, who knew what was in style? What they both concluded was that he was in his early forties, still trim, and probably didn't spend much time kicking back with a few friends and enjoying a brew or two. His face was completely clear of laugh lines.

"You two have been busy." The agent closed the file and

regarded them from across the table. "A little time with Augusto Zaza and a little spent tracking down a missing Nigerian minister that ended with a serious disturbance in a harbor." He paused for a moment before he continued. "A little time doing fieldwork at the request of one Esther Chongrak. By the way, how is the bitch these days?"

"I'm sorry," Pain replied to the last question. "Esther who?"

It had quickly become apparent to the partners that this had not been the first time their new best fed-friend had read through the files.

"I wouldn't admit to knowing her either." Buchanan nodded. "But I'm glad the little girl is now safe and out of harm's way."

Agony's foot tapped her partner's softly under the table. It wasn't a quick kick to tell him to shut the fuck up. Pain interpreted it as a sign to let the man talk since far more was going on than what appeared on the surface. He gave her foot a quick double-tap in response—*Message received*.

"It has been a long day for all of us." Agent Buchanan sighed. "I look forward to the end of it so I can take the rest of the night off and enjoy a nice breakfast in the morning."

"Instant oatmeal." Pain couldn't help himself. "With a touch of unrefined brown sugar on top?"

That comment certainly earned the under-the-table kick she gave him. He took it in stride as advice offered and received, accepted it for the reprimand it was, and fell silent.

"Freshly squeezed grapefruit juice."

The partners shrugged and neither of them made any comments about orange juice vs grapefruit juice but let the agent continue.

"The trick to fresh grapefruit juice," Buchanan stated, "is to poke a small hole in the bottom of one and squeeze it until all the juice has drained out. Then, and only then, do you slice it open, spoon out what's left of the contents, and drop them into a side-serving of fruit salad."

"It sounds like too much work to me," Pain answered and received another well-deserved kick.

"But not to me." The agent studied them. "By the time breakfast is served, we will all have learned who is the squeezer and who are the squeezies."

"Oh, crap." He was about to earn another ankle kick. "And here I am, having left my purse full of fear back at the office. Could you please have one of your team have a look for it?"

The agent gave them both a cold smile "That, Mr. Pain, first initial M, is almost amusing. But you two and I are dealing with a situation here in which the slim window for laughter has long since been slammed shut."

Agony had a quick thought that maybe it was time she and Pain should refresh their lessons in Morse Code. Under the table taps and kicks weren't quite sufficient for their needs. She didn't have time to ponder the thought, however, because a rapid knock on the door announced an agent who stuck her head in.

"Agent Buchanan?" The young woman, just out of the academy at Quantico, wasn't sure where to begin so she defaulted to chronological order. "I have a call on hold from Agent Ambrose who says it's urgent, and the lawyers are here to demand to talk to their clients."

This was one of the reasons that Special Agent Marshal Buchanan was aggrieved whenever a case brought him into the local headquarters late at night. On the midnight shift, the building was occupied by two types of agents.

Those who, after twenty or in some cases thirty years of service, had never done anything of distinction and were therefore assigned to the late shift so they could put their time in without doing too much damage until they could retire with full pension benefits. They were the antithesis of the young agents trying to earn their wings and doing their damndest to not fuck up.

The older ones were nothing more than clock-watchers. The

younger ones had often gone through so much training that they forgot the simple things. In this instance, it was one of the most basic—subjects the FBI brought in for questioning had no right to legal counsel. The agency did not run a cop-shop.

He wanted to snap a reprimand but Agent Ambrose had been deep undercover for a while now and he hadn't heard from him lately. Without a word, he snatched his file up and hurried out and to his office to take the call, leaving the late-shifters in charge of his latest acquisitions.

"Did you call a lawyer?" Agony asked her partner quickly during the brief moments while the changing of the guards took place.

"I don't have any of them on speed-dial. You?"

"Not a one."

At that point, their two attorneys entered. Twenty-seven thoughts crashed into him at the same time, none of which he had the time to explain to his partner.

"Hello, Gotong." Bora nodded his greeting. "Myself and Yejun have been requested to represent you."

Agony recognized the man immediately as the one who ran the Imperial Palace and had made them feel like welcomed guests in the sub-basement of the establishment the night they had met. The two agents who had escorted the lawyers in had been requested to remain until Special Agent Buchanan returned to continue his questioning.

"She sent you?" Pain asked and all of them except the agents understood that she was Ahjoomenoni.

"Of course." Bora nodded. "She has a vested interest in your business and as such, prefers to keep her eyes open."

"Hidden cameras in the office?" he guessed and was not pleased when the man again nodded.

"We don't need babysitting." Agony was no more pleased by the confirmation than her partner had been.

"Perhaps." Bora was not inclined to debate that point. "But in this instance, it was a good thing. Otherwise, we would not have been able to arrive so quickly."

Yejun stood to the side, his briefcase at the ready as Bora turned to the two agents who had accompanied them and asked, "Who shall I address?"

"Sorry," the older answered. "I'm not sure of the question."

"Who," he elaborated patiently, "is the agent in charge?"

"I guess that would be me, Agent Russell Williams," the same man answered as he looked at his much younger fellow agent. "I am the one with seniority."

"Oh, good. Yejun, the papers please."

Yejun set the briefcase on the table and as he opened it, Bora again addressed his clients. "What have they asked? And what have you said? She will need to know."

"So far," Pain advised his attorney, "all we have talked about is breakfast."

"Ahh, breakfast. The most important meal of the day. Hopefully, we can get this resolved quickly and enjoy one together in the morning."

He held a hand out and Yejun placed a sheet of complaints into it. Bora glanced at it briefly and addressed Agent Williams in icy tones.

"My clients have been taken in for questioning, in handcuffs and under the threat of force, but neither of them has been arrested or charged with any crimes. To effect this, the Federal Bureau of Investigations resorted to inappropriate behavior. There had been reports of gunfire at their offices and the local police had already arrived and had the situation well under control. Your fellow agents burst in—and in a most unprofessional manner, I might add—and started throwing their government badges around. This was clearly a local matter and should not have concerned anyone at the federal level."

"Well...uh, I..." Agent Williams stammered. "We," he added with a nod at the younger agent, "were not at the scene so I can't answer that."

Bora scanned his sheet again. "So you will not be named in the suit we will file for the emotional damage my extremely innocent clients suffered while being forced to kneel at gunpoint in their own offices."

Yejun withdrew another sheet and handed it to his elder.

"You will also not be personally named in a separate complaint that will seek monetary compensation for the damages done to one Ezekial Anderson's patellas when the old custodian was also forced to remain kneeling, under duress, for an unnecessary amount of time. The man may never be able to work again."

"Look..." The senior agent felt as if the ground had begun to shift and he wasn't sure how to keep his footing. "It's like I said, we weren't there."

"Let me make this very clear." Bora worked the intimidation angle hard. "I want my clients either charged or released. You said you were the agent in charge, so either charge them or let them go."

"When I said I was the agent in charge," Williams tried to clarify, "I meant that I was in charge at the moment, in this office, but only because I'm the senior agent in the room. The actual agent in charge had to step out for a minute."

"So you have wasted my time, Agent Williams. Please request the agent in charge to return immediately so he can file charges or let my clients go."

"Hello, Bora." Agent Buchanan entered and spoke from behind the attorney, who had his back to the door.

He spun toward the voice and from his expression, Pain and Agony could tell that he did not like what he saw.

"Agent Buchanan." He did not even give a slight bow as he addressed the agent.

"*Special* Agent Buchanan, as you very well know. And I am the agent in charge on this one. Very personally in charge. Do you need an escort out or do you remember the way?"

"Sorry, Gotong and Ms. Goni. I am afraid we will not be able to assist you any further tonight."

Bora handed the papers to Yejun who placed them in the briefcase, closed it, and headed toward the doorway in which Buchanan still stood.

Pain shrugged. "Hey, you tried."

"And you know how to behave. Perhaps I will be able to see you for breakfast after all."

"Don't count on it." The senior agent didn't move.

"Are we being detained now also?"

"I would be in favor of it." Buchanan finally stepped aside and let the two attorneys pass. "Agent Williams?"

"Yes, sir?"

"Will you kindly guide these gentlemen out? I would hate for them to make a wrong turn."

"Yes, sir." The older agent was glad to leave the whole scene behind him.

"How about me, sir?" the younger asked.

"And what is your name?"

"Conrad. Agent James Conrad. Second-grade."

"Well, second-grade Agent James Conrad. Can you please keep an eye out in the hallway? I would prefer to not be disturbed until I ask for assistance. I need to have a few words with my new friends here."

"Yes, sir." Agent Conrad stepped out and closed the door gently but firmly behind him.

Alone again, Buchanan faced the partners and from his look, it was obvious that the term "friends" had been a misnomer. They also saw him smile for the second time. Much like the first one he had graced them with, it was not meant to warm any hearts.

"You should be careful who you make friends with, I guess."

Special Agent Marshal Buchanan placed his folder on the table again and took his seat. "Now, where were we?"

CHAPTER FOUR

"We," Pain answered the question as Buchanan perused the file again, "were about to stand and walk out."

"I don't see that as a realistic option." The agent flipped constantly between pages of the report and made no attempt to follow the silly old eye contact routine. Pain half expected him to pull out a yellow highlighter and start marking the contents. Maybe even different colored highlighters—red for him, blue for Agony, and purple for when the names intersected.

"Why not?" He tried his best to not be overly antagonistic. "We haven't been charged, you've barely asked us any questions, and frankly, it's become a little boring. Could you please, Special Agent Buchanan, give us a little to work with here."

"We are allowed to hold you for twenty-four hours without pressing charges."

Agony took a chance and corrected him. "That's a cop policy, not a federal one."

"That's true." He shrugged the correction off, his focus still on the files. "We feds can hold you as long as we want. I don't think your lawyers will go to the press and announce that we are holding you against your will. And from what I've gathered from your files, no one will go to the cops to report you as missing persons any time soon."

"So, what does that mean?" She struggled to keep her anger under control and acknowledged ruefully that her partner wasn't the only one in the room with a temper. "You intend to simply jerk us around for twenty-four hours? Why?"

"Because I can."

He finally looked up and made eye contact with both of them. He also smiled for the third time and they realized that the reason he didn't have any laugh lines around his eyes was because the smile never reached them. His smiles ranged from cold, to calculating, to insufferable. If any of them contained anything resembling a sense of humor, it was humor that leaned toward the dark side of the spectrum.

"I must admit, though…" The smile disappeared and this seemed to add a little touch of warmth to his voice. "Together, you two have managed some quite remarkable feats. Once you get past your previous career records, it is quite impressive."

"But not impressive enough to let us go about our merry way under our own recognizance." Agony had felt a slight shift in the agent's attitude. It wasn't necessarily a good one but rather one with a little less pressure behind it.

"That would be correct. I still have questions about the alleged assault on your offices."

"You were there and saw the damage," she pointed out. "There was nothing alleged about it."

"I saw the aftermath." Buchanan's tone at least bordered on civil. "But not the actual event. For all I know, you could have shot up your own offices in order to file some kind of insurance claim."

"Seriously?" She shook her head. "You're going with that as a line of investigation?"

"I've seen it before," he stated quite matter of factly.

She had to agree since she'd seen it before too.

"But I do seriously doubt that is the case here," he added. "I honestly believe you were attacked. The question is by who and why?"

Agony seemed to be making progress with the cologne-overloaded fed and Pain kept his mouth shut as she ran with it.

"We already told you we don't know who or why."

"No, you didn't tell me that but you have now. Which is why I have agents there, even as we speak, gathering ballistics and fingerprints. The fingerprints are what I am most interested in. Several of the cases you two have been involved in could be classified as an Item of Interest to the FBI. It's not like you've investigated the average corner pickpocket, now is it?"

The partners looked at each other and nodded. He had a valid point.

"So," Special Agent Buchanan continued, "who have you pissed off enough to want to do you serious bodily harm, and might they be someone who I, as an authorized federal special agent, should be interested in?"

"Why don't you collect the fingerprints, run them through your supersized fingerprint databases, and let us go? What's the big deal?" Agony didn't hold out much hope for a positive outcome but thought it was worth the attempt.

"Did it ever occur to either of you that I might be holding you here for your protection simply out of the goodness of my heart?"

She recognized that as a line of grade-A bullshit. "That would be easier to swallow if I thought you might be in possession of a heart."

"Oh." The agent clasped his hands to his chest in mock pain "I must have a heart because I have just been stabbed in it and the hurt is almost unbearable."

"Will we be done with this game anytime soon?" Pain's patience with the agent's routine was running out. His partner had succeeded as the good-PI and it was now his turn to play bad-PI. "Whether it's for our good or not to be held here is up to us—as US citizens—to decide, not an agent who in my eyes falls far short of being *special*."

"Oh." Buchanan moaned. "Another dagger straight to what must be my heart. You two are ruthless."

"No." He ignored the histrionics. "What we are is tired."

"As am I." Buchanan suddenly turned serious. "I don't know who you pissed off, or how many federal investigations those people may be under and how many of those investigations you two may have inadvertently interfered with. Until I get more information, the best I can do is to acknowledge how tired you are and offer you both accommodations for the night."

He walked to the door and stepped into the hallway to speak to Agent Second-grade James Conrad.

"That was smooth," Agony whispered sharply while they had a moment alone.

"Something more is going on here," he responded quietly. "I don't know what the hell it is, but we are being dragged into it and I don't like it even a little."

"It hasn't ranked high on my list of the top one-hundred nights in my life either," she informed him through gritted teeth and sighed as she tried to push her irritation aside. "What do we know so far?"

"Nothing." Pain suspected that they only had a few more seconds of privacy left. "Except that Bora and Buchanan have run into each other before."

"And where Bora goes?"

"Ahjoomenoni is somewhere in the background pulling the strings," he confirmed bluntly.

"Aw, man." Agony had begun to gain a deeper understanding

of her sweet little old landlady. "And here I thought her and I would end up being besties."

"He said twenty-four hours, right?"

"That's what I heard," she agreed and added, "If you can take the word of a fed."

"It's all we have at the moment."

Buchanan entered the room with two agents—James Conrad and the young female whose name they didn't catch when she had interrupted the initial round of interrogation.

"See you mañana." Pain gave their traditional parting words each night when they headed to their separate abodes as he stood and walked calmly toward Agent Conrad.

"Mañana," Agony echoed as she stood slowly to let young Agent Whatever-her-name-was guide her to her holding cell.

"I'll check in now and then," the special agent promised—or threatened—as they passed him. "I want to make sure our honored guests are treated properly."

Agent Buchanan was true to his word. He did visit them in their holding cells but only once later that night while the moon slid across the sky on its nightly circuit.

Pain had spent many nights in more uncomfortable confines. He had a concrete bed along one wall with a thin mattress, the standard lidless toilet, and a small stainless-steel sink to either rinse his hands or to cup some water in them from the faucet to stop his throat from becoming too dry.

By this point, he was used to all kinds of discomfort while on assignments and since he'd come back Stateside and lived rough while on his quest. The one thing he had probably missed the most often during those times was the luxury of a quick sip of water late at night. He could sleep through damn near any distraction, but to have a dry throat late at night, when only one sip of water would have eased him to sleep again, was something he had never adjusted to.

His cell opened within an hour after he'd checked in. His best guess was that it was around three am when the special agent entered.

"So," Pain asked and remained stretched on his thin mattress, "is this how the night will go? Break the sleep cycle every hour but vary it by fifteen minutes either way in case I'm counting seconds in my head until your next arrival?"

Buchanan didn't speak. He merely leaned against a wall and observed him.

"Oh, I see," Pain muttered after five minutes had passed. "The strong silent type. I hear some women go for that."

Another five minutes of silence passed and he tried to let the man down easy, "It's not that I don't enjoy your wit and charm during these conversations we have, but I will go to sleep now. As you stand there and observe, if you see any evidence of me having an erotic dream, it will be of three vixens I once spent a weekend with on St. Croix—and no, we don't need to turn the foursome into a five-some, but I will give them your regards."

The agent left as quietly as he'd entered without having spoken a word.

"Curiouser and curiouser," he mumbled as he drifted off to pursue the babes from St. Croix.

Agony had difficulty adapting to her overnight accommodations. During her cop days, she had always been the one on the outside of the holding cells. After she had closed the doors on the occupants she had placed in them, her duty had been done and she slept soundly because she believed that for at least one night, she had taken someone bad off the street.

Granted, some of those she had locked up overnight had eventually been proven innocent and for that, she had suffered occasional pangs of guilt for the uncomfortable night they had spent in their cells. She had consoled herself with the knowledge that the bad had far outnumbered the innocent and she could live with the percentages.

Now, however, being on the other side of the door, she realized that the innocent didn't give a shit about percentages. She paced and cursed under her breath because she didn't want anyone listening on the other side of the door to know she was reacting badly to her confinement.

Fucking Pain. He is probably as relaxed as could be while he occupies his mind with chess moves. She stretched on the threadbare mattress, held her hands out above her in the darkness, and envisioned one hand holding a chess piece that looked like a horse kicking the shit out of a king.

"Neigh, neigh," she whispered. "Take *that* Mister King! Come on, Ms. Queen. Hop on my back and together, we'll get out of this shit-hole. Oh, thank you, Horsie. Giddy-up!"

She had almost distracted herself enough to sleep when the cell door opened. Instantly wide awake, she reached instinctively for her baton. When awareness of where she was returned, she did a couple of quick flexes and stood. Her MMA muscle memories at the ready, she backed against a wall in her cell so that she wouldn't have to worry about anyone coming at her from behind.

A moment later, her nose kicked in and let her know, without any question, that her visitor was the possessor of the odoriferous offense.

"Agent Buchanan." She intentionally left out the special. "Do your parents know that you are up past your bedtime?"

Her taunt was greeted by silence.

"If I shouted rape, do you think anyone would hear me and run to my rescue? Sorry, that's a stupid question. I would need to fill a form out in triplicate and submit it so it could be presented to a committee before anyone would act on it."

Again, she received no response.

"Fuck this shit. I'm going back to bed now. I was dreaming about horsies, not horsies' asses."

She walked to her concrete bed and lay on her side, which would leave both her arms and legs free to strike out at different angles if necessary.

As before when he'd entered Pain's room, Special Agent Marshal Buchanan left her room as quietly and speechlessly as he'd entered. He had learned everything he'd needed to know.

Agony was left without a clue as to what the agent's intentions had been but was fairly sure they were aimed more at intimidation than sexual assault. It would be daylight soon, and if he was true to his word, they still had a dozen hours or so before they would be released. She wanted to get in at least two hours' sleep and tried to recapture the adventures Horsie and Queenie were about to get into. It worked surprisingly well. Whether it was the mind game she played or sheer exhaustion didn't matter. She had three hours of solid sleep before the morning routine started.

What both partners endured the next day was essentially the same. No food that resembled breakfast slop was slid under the door and no one came in and bombarded either of them with questions.

What was more frustrating was that no one entered their doors to answer any questions either. When the day finally reached what they judged to be noon, the routine was growing old. Silence was their only companion. They spent considerable time wondering and worrying about each other's well-being but they were ignored, isolated not only from each other but from all other human contact.

Lunch was also a meal that failed to make an appearance.

Neither one of them raised any kind of a fuss or ruckus, as tempting as it was to bang on their doors and shout demands. If this was the way the game would be played, they would master it, wait for the twenty-four hours to pass, and see if Agent Buchanan kept his word.

Pain passed his time by pulling his boots off and rolling his socks into balls to work on his hand-eye coordination by juggling the two socks and two boots. The four objects had different weights and drop ratios. He had never tried four-object juggling before but was pleased with the progress he made.

Agony also passed the time working on some moves. Hers involved rolling and folding her thin mattress into various compact forms, then tossing it into the air to see how many punches and kicks she could deliver to it as it unfolded and landed on the floor.

Neither of them had another visit from Agent Buchanan, but the twenty-four hours must have passed because late that afternoon, they were released from their cells and taken to the receiving area, where all their possessions were returned. They were then escorted onto the street and bid fond farewells by agents whose names they didn't bother to learn.

The fresh air felt good and they stood for a minute to breathe it in.

"How many visits from Buchanan did you get?" Pain was the first to ask as they walked through the fed plaza toward the street where they could hail a cab.

"One," she answered. "You?"

"The same. I hate to admit it, but I'm not sure what game is being played here."

"There you are!" Buchanan called in a hail and well-met tone of voice as he rushed to catch up to them. "Sorry about all that," he apologized. "You both know how it is when you have to answer to superiors who call the shots."

"Who are you?" Agony asked. "And what have you done with Special Agent Buchanan?"

"Yeah," he admitted, "I did come across a little hard and heavy. Sorry. I hope there are no hard feelings." He slapped both their shoulders in a Hardy, we're all friends here kind of way. "I gotta run back inside. A fed's day is never done. We'll be in touch and thanks. You've both been great sports about all this."

Agent Buchanan hurried away and vanished into the heart of FBI darkness. The evening rush hour was winding down and while they waited to flag a cab down, they acknowledged that neither of them had been offered anything to eat by their federal hosts and both could go for a nice meal. They also had to return to their office to see how much of it was left. Sadly, it was currently during the hours that Pasha's and Masha's delis weren't open.

"It might take us long enough to clean up," Pain pointed out, "that Masha's might be open by the time we're done."

"Oh, fuck us!"

"What?" He wasn't used to his partner being so pissed off about having missed a couple of meals. "We'll find a street vendor and at least pick up enough to carry us over until the cleaning's done."

"It's not the food." She spun and looked at the fed's headquarters. "What do you think all that playing friendly and shoulder slaps were about?"

"I hadn't thought about it," Pain admitted. "But you're right. He didn't seem like a touchy-feely kind of guy before."

"But now?" She wanted to see if she could guide him to his conclusion and compare it with what she had come up with. "Right here in a public space in front of the fed's local headquarters?"

She could tell by his darkening glare and the way his fists began to clench and unclench that they would soon be on the same page.

"We spent twenty-four hours in there," he summarized, "away from all prying eyes and have come out unscathed with Agent Buchanan treating us like we were old college roommates."

"And acting like that in full view of anyone who might be watching," she added, the same page having been reached. "We don't know what the history between him and Ahjoomenoni is, but from Bora and his associate's reaction, we can assume it's not a pleasant one. I'm seriously considering the fact that we may have been royally set up and screwed over because it now looks as if we've spent the last twenty-four hours cooperating with him."

"There is one way to find out." Pain started toward the building, his stride strong and aggrieved. "I'm gonna do a little Royal Rumbling."

"No, you're not!" Agony caught his arm and spun him toward the street. "If you need to do some damage, go and pick on an innocent delivery truck. Otherwise, you'll end up putting several people in the hospital and yourself in jail on some serious assault and battery charges. We'll have to be much smarter about this."

He turned full circle a few times while the evening shadows crept between the high-rises.

"What the hell are you doing?" she demanded.

"Trying to find which way is north."

"What? Do you plan to walk to Canada?"

"All right." He settled a little. "Maybe that's not the best plan. We need to go to Ahjoomenoni and tell her everything. We know she had cameras or at least listening devices in our office, but even she isn't powerful enough to be able to set bugs up in Fed Central. We need to fill her in on what happened during our time there."

"I said be smart, dumbass." She resisted the temptation to try to smack some sense into his thick skull. "That does not mean walk into the house of someone who will bury us in her basement."

"We have Special Agent Marshal Buchanan on one side and the most dangerous woman I've ever met on the other. The simple truth is that she is one of the very few people I have ever feared. A long stroll to the Canadian border sounds more and more attractive."

CHAPTER FIVE

Agony admitted that the Canadian national anthem was much easier to sing than the US's. That said, she had no desire to live where it was common for the snow to begin falling before Halloween and often linger until sometime after school let out for the summer.

"All right." Pain sighed. "Let's hold off on visiting our office and check in to pay our respects to our landlady first."

"Pay our respects? Or beg for mercy?" She couldn't help a little snark.

"We'll simply have to multi-task."

Unfortunately, plans for their evening's destinations being what they were, their office—as well as Bertha—were in the opposite direction from their apartments above Kwan's, which was where they would no doubt find Ahjoomenoni. Kwan's was a Five-star Korean restaurant to its patrons and the business offices of a ruthless empress to those who were more familiar with its owner's history.

Bertha, being the faithful vehicle she was, would have to wait for them to retrieve her as soon as they could. She was very patient that way. They managed to flag a cab down, neither of them being ride-lifts kind of people, and arrived in front of Kwan's during the middle of the dinner rush.

They decided that maybe after having spent twenty-four hours in holding cells, they should both shower, freshen up, and wait for the evening business to be over before they made an appearance in front of the venerable Ahjoomenoni. Those plans were immediately adjusted when they found a man standing to the side of the door that led to the stairway to their apartments above.

He didn't look like hired muscle on a mission but rather like a well-dressed middle-aged Korean man waiting for his dinner date to arrive and did not want to appear so rude as to head into the restaurant ahead of his companion, who was running a few minutes late.

"Your hostess is awaiting your arrival," the man said as they passed him on their way to the door.

From the calm but firm tone in his voice, they knew he was not holding a cell phone conversation with a long-lost cousin or a dinner date who was held up in traffic. He was addressing them and only them.

"Perhaps," Pain replied, "you would be so kind as to guide us to her presence?"

"That is a request I can honor."

Without another word, the gentleman led them into the restaurant and into one of the two most private dining spaces, both of which—if Pain's memory served—were reserved at least three months in advance. Luxury abounded in those two rooms and each held one round table that would seat only six.

The entree options were limited to a short list of items that were not listed on Kwan's official menu. They consisted of delicacies that, while they didn't qualify as endangered species, were not readily available in the country in which the restaurant operated.

When the partners were guided into the room, Ahjoomenoni

sat alone at the table, her dinner having either not arrived yet or been finished and cleared away due to their late arrival.

Pain began his customary bow before speaking. Agony, having become accustomed to the tradition, made a bow to their hostess as well.

Neither bow was allowed to finish as both the partner's heads were suddenly forced onto the tabletop by guards who had stood in the shadows. The unmistakable feel of the end of gun barrels made their presence known above the back of their necks.

Their heads were pressed sideways on the tabletop, with other peoples' guns at the ready, never anyone's favorite position. At least they were facing each other and only inches apart, which gave Agony a chance to whisper, "I'm waiting for that special relationship you have with her to invoke some understanding any second now."

"Cut me some slack, will ya? At least we're not in the basement yet."

"No, asshole, but I can see the stairs from here."

"She's your BFF," Pain reminded her. "You talk to her."

"According to you, I haven't earned the right to talk to her yet," she reminded him.

"When was the last time you listened to anything I ever said?"

"You shouted 'duck' once and I followed that command as promptly as I could, oh master," she snapped, her eyes staring daggers at him.

"And you haven't once thanked me for that."

"Maybe that's because if I hadn't ducked, I would have been instantly put out of my misery and wouldn't have to be stuck dealing with you anymore. Have you ever thought of that?"

"Ip dakchyeo!" Their hostess almost raised her voice.

"What does that mean?" Agony tried a lower whisper.

"It means it would be wise for us to both shut the fuck up."

"Oh."

Five seconds of silence followed without a peep from either of them. That seemed to be enough to satisfy their hostess and the gun barrels were removed from contact with their heads. They were allowed to stand and take their seats, fully aware that the men with the guns remained quietly in the background.

Another day and another interrogation. They both hoped that this wouldn't become part of their daily routine.

"I have already enjoyed my dinner and dessert," Ahjoomenoni was kind enough to inform them, "so you need not worry about causing damage to my appetite. Who shall speak the truth to me first?"

"We shall both speak the truth to you." Pain nodded. "But I will volunteer to speak first."

"Is that acceptable to you, partner of Pain?" she asked with no twinkle of their having bonded woman to woman in her eye.

"It is." Agony nodded.

"First," Ahjoomenoni turned to Pain, "tell me what I already know."

"You know," he began cautiously and courteously, "that you have had our offices wired for either sound and or video since shortly after we moved in."

The woman merely nodded with neither an apology nor an explanation, so he continued.

"You also know that we were released from the FBI field office and were warmly congratulated by Agent Buchanan as he sent us on our way."

Again, Ahjoomenoni nodded but added, "Special Agent Buchanan. He is very touchy if one forgets to include the special."

It was a statement that confirmed to the partners that some still waters ran deep between their landlady and the agent. They both despised one of them and Agony was learning why Pain feared the other.

"What you also know," he added and resumed the conversation, "is that I have no love for the feds and that twenty-four hours in custody would not change that. I do not know what his end game is, but holding us in custody was only a small part of it. The only thing Agony or I spoke to him about was how tedious it was to be in his presence."

"This was while you were together," Ahjoomenoni clarified for them. "But after Bora and his associate left, I am certain that you two were not left to share a room. What happened after you were separated?"

"I can't speak for my partner," he stated to finish his narrative, "but he only came into my cell once, for no reason other than to disturb my sleep pattern. He asked no questions, and after I offered a couple of harmless observations about his nocturnal habits, he left. I did not see him again until after we had been released and he caught up with us in the plaza, acting for all the world to see that we were his two best friends." He gave a slight bow and added, "But that last part you no doubt already know."

"Yes." The woman sighed. "It was quite a performance but I see no Oscar in his future."

She turned her attention to Agony. "Tell me, partner of Pain, how did your twenty-four hours in custody go?"

"About the same," she answered in a tone that held nothing but respect. "Except that for many of the hours I spent alone, I didn't spend endless hours running through chess moves in my head to relieve the boredom like I assume my partner did."

"And what did you do as you endured the boredom?"

Careful, partner. Pain tried to subliminally message her.

Agony had either missed or chosen to ignore the warning. "I spent the time coming to the conclusion that Agent Buchanan wasn't after us. He was more interested in you. To use a phrase my partner and his chess-fixation can understand, he simply used us as pawns in a game that has been played out for a long time before we were placed on the board to be used as sacrifices."

"That is quite an interesting analogy," Ahjoomenoni conceded.

"If we must be pawns," she replied, pleased by the compliment, "we would rather be used as your pawns."

"You did not care for him?" the sweet, deadly landlady asked.

"Nor his cologne." She shook her head at the memory. "He is odiferous in every way."

"With that assessment," the woman nodded, "I agree."

With a wave of her hand, Ahjoomenoni dismissed the men with the guns and the three were left alone. Agony's senses let her begin to relax.

Pain's senses sent him to high alert. He'd had many more dealings with the woman before. *But hey,* he hoped, *maybe girl-power-sisterhood does count for something.* He kept his unease to himself and his mouth shut, determined to only open it if requested to do so.

"Greetings, Ahjoomenoni," Agony addressed her landlady and bowed her head. "I realize that I am young and sometimes presumptuous. I, as AG, have never meant to disrespect you by calling you AJ. I am simply Alicia Goni, a name with no history other than what I have made of it. You, on the other hand, are Ahjoomenoni. I do not know what that name means in your native language, but I am sure it is one of distinction."

"It is not a matter of distinction. It is a matter of recognition."

The simple statement left her wondering if Ahjoomenoni was her name or her title. She would have to remember to ask Pain about that some other time.

"First," the Korean mob boss continued, "I believe your accounts of having given the agent no information. This belief is made easier because you have nothing to give him of me that is of any importance to him."

"Thank you for your faith." Pain nodded and resumed his silence, worried about what news second, or third, or fourth might bring and wondering which one would end up with them tossed into a basement. He did not want to be slow-roasted, sliced, and served with a variety of dipping sauces as a specialty menu item.

"Second," Ahjoomenoni informed them, "I am not one of the agent's favorite people. He has made this very clear for a number of years now. The man has been what you call a thorn in my side. The kind of thorn that only a dedicated *ssibal-saekki* can be."

"*Ssibal-saekki?*" Agony looked at Pain for some assistance.

"Mother-fucking son of a bitch would be a fairly accurate translation," he told her.

"Just so, yes," the woman agreed. "As a baby, he should have been placed in a Kimchi pot, buried, and forgotten about."

Nope, Agony thought, *the landlady and the agent are in no danger of reconciling any time soon.*

"I have, as you know," Ahjoomenoni said to Pain, "traveled far and not in a distance that can be measured in miles. I have made more than one enemy along the way." She shrugged slightly. "But that is merely the nature of business. This agent, however, is the only one who has come even close to shutting down any of my enterprises. It is as if he has a personal vendetta against me that goes beyond reasonable expectations."

The statement or admission took Pain by surprise. The agent had more balls than he had given him credit for.

"That," he acknowledged, "makes him a very formidable opponent. Is there any way we can assist? Perhaps if you told us the source of the vendetta, Agony and I can work to erase it."

"Sadly, I honestly do not know."

That bothersome statement left him even more concerned. He had seldom heard her speak this way.

"I have spent much effort digging into the agent's past, wondering where we may have crossed paths in such a way that would justify the determination with which he has targeted me and my various enterprises. Despite this, I have come up with nothing that I could use as leverage to perhaps dissuade him from pursuing his investigations. He is what you call squeaky-clean, and that makes him seem the kind of man who would make a perfect martyr."

"In other words," he concluded, "there is no way to remove him without drawing an even larger amount of unwanted attention."

"This is correct." She was not surprised that he was able to summarize her problems so succinctly. "He will continue until he chooses to no longer do so."

"But what if we looked into him ourselves?" Agony suggested and didn't notice her partner's quick grimace. "Maybe we can find something that has eluded you so far."

Ahjoomenoni responded with a soft rebuke. "Someday in the future, that may be an option. But for now, I have already decided on my course of action."

"But you have already stated that you can't kill him." She was missing Pain's mental telepathy as he tried to tell her to shut the fuck up. "What other options are there?"

"I have decided on isolation. It will be the best tool to stave off his continued toxic groping into my enterprises. He is only one man and not a friendly one, but he is still only one man on a one-man crusade. Unless he can convince his superiors to form an organized task force, the damage he can do to my organization is limited."

"But what if he manages to form a task force?"

Drop it, drop it, drop it! He closed his eyes and put his fingers to his temples, thinking maybe that would help his telepathic advice to be able to power through to his partner.

"You have met the man. His being able to pull together a task force is not a concern. He is not that persuasive. But sadly, this brings me to my third point."

Don't be basement, don't be basement, don't be basement. Pain worked this one mentally very hard.

"Anyone who has come to the agent's attention," Ahjoomenoni explained, "which the two of you have managed to do, will have to be treated as poison fruit. I must cut off any and all branches that might lead back to me. This way, I can be assured that this son of a wanton woman will not be able to get into anything too sensitive or problematic for my purposes and I can limit the damage he can do to me to a minimum. Perhaps he will eventually become bored and find someone else to focus his attention on. Which means, I am afraid, that the two of you can no longer remain in my good graces. As I stated, for however long the agent is still looking around my orchards, all branches of poisoned fruit must be severed."

Pain was thankful that a basement wasn't in their immediate future, at least by Ahjoomenoni's hand, but he did need a little more information.

"We accept your logic and understand your conclusions, Ahjoomenoni. You are being very gracious by informing us. But please let us know, for clarification purposes, does cutting all ties," he ventured to ask, "also mean your investment in P & A Investigations?"

"That is correct." She almost sounded apologetic. "The loan has already been severed and the account set up for you to draw on it has been closed."

The partners could deal with that but exchanged a glance.

"And our apartments?" Agony was the first one brave enough to ask.

"I did say all," The landlady's voice was suddenly ice. "Does all mean something else on the planet from which you hail?"

CHAPTER SIX

Pain and Agony were escorted out of their rather disconcerting meeting with Ahjoomenoni. To their surprise, they weren't taken out the way they'd come in but along a short, dark hallway. The good news was that it didn't lead to a basement.

The bad news was that they hadn't had time to discuss how much time they might be allowed to clean out their apartments. Before they could even ask, they stepped into the alley behind the building and learned that all their meager possessions had already been removed from the building and now sat in four large garbage bags next to the dumpsters. A half-dozen raggedy folks had already begun to sort through them.

The news in the dumpster-divers' network traveled fast given their lack of social networking.

"Excuse us, people!" Agony held up her PI's license that in the dim lights of the alley could easily pass for a cop's badge, especially since she sounded like a cop. "We would like to thank whoever phoned this in. Those bags match the description of the B & E we were looking into."

"Whoever the thieves were," a man called in a gravelly voice, "they musta made off with all the good stuff 'cause there ain't shit here."

"But sometimes shit holds clues," she informed them. "So please, everyone, back off and find another alley so we can go about our jobs."

"I'm good at sorting through shit," another man informed her while he scrutinized one of Pain's favorite shirts. "Maybe you can hire me as a consultant or something."

"You heard the detective." Pain stepped forward and spoke as authoritatively as he could. "It's time to find another place to be."

"Sure." The shit-sorting specialist tossed the shirt onto the bag he'd found it in. "Nothing here is worth our time anyway."

They waited as the small crowd wandered off.

Agony sighed. "There is nothing like having your entire life's worldly possessions studied and rejected by such a high-society panel of judges."

Pain picked the shirt up and held it out. "Is this shirt that bad?"

"Not if you're an eighty-year-old named Ralph who's trying to impress the ladies at the shuffleboard courts in Florida."

He took another look at the shirt through fresh eyes and decided that he might never go clothes shopping without a consultant again.

"I'll keep an eye on our pile of treasures." He began to shove things into the bags. "If you'll catch a cab and retrieve Bertha."

"That would sound like a sweet deal," she answered, "except I'm a little low on cash at the moment."

He pulled his wallet out and handed her a twenty.

"Thanks." She started toward the street at the end of the alley and stopped. "You don't carry a wallet."

"I know." He had always admired her observational skills. "But Jiho does—or at least did until he bent me over a table and put a gun to my head while I picked his pocket. Now, how about you get a move on so we can also use his plastic to get a room or two before he realizes it's missing."

"I'll be back in a jif."

Pain watched her hurry away, removed the two hundred in cash, and examined the four credit cards. He lined them up in the order he suspected their limits were, from lowest to highest. With the cards sorted, he was ready when his partner arrived in Bertha a half-hour later.

They tossed all four of their bags in and he directed her to a nearby no-tell motel.

"There is no way I'm staying here tonight," she told him firmly as she pulled into the parking lot.

"Neither am I." He agreed with her assessment because it looked like it often rented rooms out by the hour as opposed to a day. "But I'm drunk and you'll follow me when I go inside. You will stand outside the office window looking like a working girl who simply wants to get her current customer done with as quickly as possible."

"Will you explain?"

"As soon as I get back from renting a room for Jiho."

Her partner went inside. Agony stood outside the office window while he did a very good drunken pantomime and pointed at her. The clerk behind the desk didn't bother to ask for ID. He rang the room up and wished Pain a pleasant good night.

"You used to work vice. Choose the next hotel that's on the vice radar."

"You said you would explain," she reminded him as she put Bertha in gear and headed to the Travelers Rest.

"I've never enjoyed having a gun at the back of my head," he summarized briefly, "but I did not want to upset our hostess. Jiho has a tendency to enjoy a drink or two and a lady or three. We'll simply spread his wealth around so that by the time he sobers up tomorrow, he'll have a difficult time remembering what he got up to tonight."

They repeated the routine at the Travelers Rest, except she rang the bell to get the night clerk's attention away from whoever he was talking to on his cell.

Pain braced himself against the doorframe as she presented the card and rented a room.

"I should have gone undercover more often when I worked vice," she declared as they returned to Bertha and proceeded to their next stop. "I make a convincing hooker."

"How did I do as a drunken john?" he asked and wondered if she thought his acting abilities were equal to hers.

"I think the clerk wasn't worried about how hard I would have to work. His only concern was if I would be able to get you into the room and onto the bed before you collapsed in a stupor, preferably not in the little lobby where he might have to mop your vomit up."

"Excellent."

Now that she understood the strategy, she already had the next destination in mind and drove to The Promenade Palace. Pain noted that it was slightly more upscale than their first two stops.

"You can sit this one out," she informed him and hurried inside and directly to the desk.

"Hello, Vincent." Agony greeted the night clerk as an old friend.

"Oh, no, no." The man sighed. "You people used us only two months ago. I thought we were on a four-month rotation."

"What can I say?" She handed him the third of Jiho's cards. "Business has been good."

"Good for you maybe," Vincent replied, "but every time you use my hotel for a sting, I lose a quarter of my business for a month."

She hadn't been there in three years but was relieved to know that the rotating vice-squad room rental was still being used. Better yet, Vincent hadn't heard that she was no longer on the force, which also worked in her favor as he ran the card without any further questions and assigned her the key to room 220, which was the usual one. It was at the end of the second floor and had easy access for a keycard holder to enter the room and lead a john into it. As soon as money exchanged hands, the bust went down without disturbing too many guests.

"That went well?" her partner asked as she slid behind Bertha's wheel.

"Sometimes, it's good to have friends in low places." She smiled. "Give me a sec. We still need a place to crash."

He had intended to explain their next stop but honored her wishes and remained silent.

It had been a while since she'd abandoned—or maybe escaped was more apt—her previous apartment due to a lack of security. None of the issues she'd experienced had anything to do with Jamal down the hallway, who she knew had always had a slight crush on her. He was one of the good ones and she trusted him enough to know that he would be willing to give them both a space to crash for a night while they got their bearings and would ask for nothing in return.

"Hello?" a sleepy female voice answered.

"Sorry," Agony replied. "I must have dialed the wrong number. I was trying to reach Raphael."

"Jamal?" She heard the sleepy, sweet-sounding voice address whoever was in the bed next to her. "We don't know any Raphaels, do we?"

She hung up. Jamal might have finally found someone who deserved him.

"I was about to tell you," Pain informed his partner, who briefly indulged a sweet smile at the idea of future bliss for her friend, "that I have already reserved us a room for the night."

"A room? Where?" She wasn't sure which less than stellar hotel they would have to settle for.

"At the Mondalee."

"I won't raid our Eddie stash!" She was pissed. The Eddie stash was their little secret from a recent job and they had agreed that they would only use it for dire emergencies. "And neither of us can afford a night at the Mondalee."

"I agree." He held up the platinum card he'd saved for last. "But Jiho can. I have already booked the room. That's why we made our three earlier stops at the other motels. It will be up to him to try to sort out how many places he visited tonight, and who knows how many calls to his credit card companies to find out how much he spent. But of course, he won't start doing that until he comes back to consciousness from his nightly stupor and realizes that he is no longer in possession of his wallet."

"And what is our story when we get there?" she asked as she turned onto the street that would take them to the hotel.

"We have returned on a long international flight from Morroco. I made the reservation while we were still in the air and somehow, between the airline losing our luggage and too many drinks being served for free while flying first-class, the idiot you are taking care of managed to misplace his wallet. We hope we had an honest limo driver who will report having found it when he cleans the vehicle at the end of his shift."

"That may be one of the dumbest stories I've ever heard." She felt obligated to inform him of this.

"I will acknowledge that assessment." He nodded. "But anyone who keeps track of what anyone in Hollywood is up to will know that Dwayne The Rock Johnson recently finished three months of shooting an adventure film set on location in the Sahara Desert that Morocco borders."

"This may be the exact moment," Agony informed him, "that I start to believe you are truly and certifiably insane."

Pain ignored the comment and continued the narrative. "The Rock's stuntman double had to take a few more falls and tumbles than were initially planned for in order to please the obsessive director and was too sore to stay for the wrap-party. He wanted to get home to his personal chiropractor, but the pain meds and the drinks may have been an unwise combination. It is a good thing that the studio assigned the stuntman a personal assistant to make sure he arrived home safely."

"That settles it." She shook her head. "You are utterly and completely certifiable."

"Slap a magnetic *Delivery Specialist* sign on the side of Bertha and let's go get us a room."

It took her four minutes to find and affix the proper magnetic sign. Three minutes later, Agony pulled into the drive in front of the Mondalee and assisted The Rock's stunt double out of the multi-purpose minivan.

"Are you..." the head valet started to ask when he saw Pain being assisted out of Bertha's passenger seat.

"No," he mumbled in a very credible pretense of being half-medicated and half-drunk, "I'm not. I'm his stunt double. Dwayne's still in Morocco wrapping up a few scenes."

"Please," Agony implored as she placed one of his arms around her shoulders to be better able to help guide him into the hotel. "Can you please park this so that I can get him to his room quickly and quietly?"

She handed the valet the keys.

"They will be waiting right here on our key board when you need them again," he assured her.

"Thank you." She guided her stumbling partner into the hotel as cell phones were brandished to take frantic pictures.

When they reached the front desk, she repeated the reservation number Pain had given her and they were soon surrounded by half a dozen late-night staff members who assisted them to their room and snuck in a dozen selfies just in case.

There was enough money on Jiho's platinum card for them to afford a two-bedroom suite. Once they'd stepped inside and managed to close the door, she collapsed into a chair. "What the hell? How did we pull that off?"

"Hey, I'm the Rock." He shrugged.

"No, you're not," she reminded him.

"Right." He opened the mini-fridge and pulled out two overly expensive small bottles of Chardonnay and handed one to her. "I'm his stunt double."

"No." She corrected him again. "You are not that either."

"Sshhh." He uncapped his bottle and raised it in a mock toast. "They don't know that. As far as they know, they helped a celebrity get into his room while he was trying to stay incognito. Sometimes, we have to allow people their illusions."

His stomach punctuated that with a rumble to remind them that neither of them had eaten anything in well over twenty-four hours. Ahjoomenoni had not only left them homeless but she had also left them hungry. The dining room was closing in an hour, so Pain called room service and ordered a New York Sirloin for himself and per his partner's request, Alaskan salmon. For sidedishes, they chose one of every option on the menu.

"Jiho, The Rock, and the stunt double all have a reputation of being able to put a large amount of food away," he said after he'd placed the order.

"It's a damn shame that none of them will be here to enjoy it."

"Is it my fault that they didn't RSVP to the invitation?"

It also occurred to them that they were wearing the same clothes they'd worn since they'd spent half a day with the city's record clerk before they returned to their office. There had been no time or opportunity to change prior to the attack that was followed by twenty-four hours in Special Agent Marshal Buchanan's custody and Ahjoomenoni's dismissal of them.

"I won't go down to Bertha simply for a change of clothes." Agony sighed.

Fortunately, the Mondalee was of the high-class style of hotels that provided luxurious monogrammed bathrobes in each suite. "You wait for the food," she told him, "while I shower."

Her long, hot scrub finished, she emerged from her side of the suite feeling almost human again and enveloped in the monogrammed robe. Pain had the food set out at the small dinette table and they dug in, each of them availing themselves of another small bottle of wine from the mini-fridge.

"Options?" he asked after they had finished the main course.

"We don't have many at the moment." She managed to sound both worried and satisfied at the same time. The salmon had been excellent. "We are on the shit-lists of an FBI agent and a very scary former landlady."

"My money is on the landlady eventually coming out on top." Pain offered his opinion with quiet certainty. "She is, after all, Ahjoomenoni and Agent Buchanan is...well, his rank may officially be special agent, but I don't think he is special enough to take her down."

Agony took her last sip of the wine. "But until he is dealt with, we will be non-existent, or worse, in Ahjoomenoni's world. We need to go after the agent." She yawned. "But how do we go about that?"

"How is not the immediate question," he answered, stifled his yawn, stretched, and stood. "The immediate question is when, and the answer to that is after a good night's sleep. Mañana?" He wandered to his room.

"Mañana," she agreed. "It has to be better than whatever the fuck the last two days have been."

"Hey, hon," Dwayne told his wife the next day while they relaxed in their weekend getaway cabin in Montana and he scrolled through his phone's news feeds. "Look where I was yesterday."

"Not bad for an imposter." She scanned the feeds and poured him a second cup of coffee, and they leaned back to watch the sun rise over the Rockies. "But I think I'll stick with the original."

CHAPTER SEVEN

After a decent night's sleep, the partners were tempted to order a room service breakfast but decided against it. They hadn't completely formalized their list of rules yet, but one of the primary ones was to never stay in the same place too long, especially when they used someone else's credit card to pay for it.

Agony had taken her previous day's clothes into the shower with her the night before. She was capable of multi-tasking when necessary and had washed and rinsed them and also showered herself clean. They had dried completely where they had hung over the shower rod so she felt at least reasonably clean. *Pain? Who knows how Pain feels when it comes to personal hygiene?*

She retrieved Bertha and pulled up in front of the Mondalee so he could slide hastily into the shotgun seat. They'd had enough of the wannabe paparazzi the night before and did their best to slip out quietly. The slipping out quietly part went well, but the where to go to part was still up for discussion.

Until the question was resolved, she chose a northward route, a strategy of her partner's she had learned to appreciate when no specific destination was on the agenda.

"Bagels or donuts?" she asked as she shifted in her seat.

"It's not a donut day," he answered firmly. They had considerable thinking and planning to do and the last thing they needed was a quick sugar rush followed by a crash.

"Oh!" Her voice lifted with sudden enthusiasm. "I know this hood. Next stop, Frinkell's." She eased her foot off the gas for a minute and asked, "You still have a little spare change left, right?"

Pain slid his hand into a pocket. "Will a twenty cover it?"

"With change left over."

"Then breakfast is on Jiho."

Agony snatched the twenty. After a couple of quick turns, she pulled into the drive-thru lane of one of the three Frinkell locations that were spread thinly throughout the city. She ordered a half-bag of assorted bagels, one of each of the three cream cheese sides, and two cups of black coffee, which was the only way Frinkell's served it.

Once the order had been paid for and handed through the window, she moved ahead and parked in an open space.

"Sorry," she explained. "I don't like to eat, think, drink, and drive all at the same time."

"A very wise rule." Pain nodded as he put the Styrofoam cups in their appropriate holders between the seats to let them cool for a minute and turned his attention to the bagels.

As was his habit, he chose the most loaded ones. Agony was thrilled to find a blueberry included in the selection and pounced on the sweet cream cheese topping.

They devoured their first bagels and washed them down with the now hot but not tongue-burning coffee before she resumed the conversation from the night before.

"In order to get back into Ahjoomenoni's good graces, we need to find a way to relieve her of a specific annoyance, correct?"

"Correct," Pain agreed, "and as much as I might prefer an up-close and personal broken neck, followed by a quick body dump in the river, that's probably not our wisest choice of action."

"I had begun to wonder if I'd ever hear you utter another sensible sentence."

"It must be the coffee." He took another sip. "Now this is the good stuff."

She had known he would like it. "I think we should start by focusing on the annoyance," she told him as she searched through the bag and snagged a cinnamon-raisin. They remained silent while she slathered it with what was left of her sweet cream and before she bit into it, she added, "But not in a way that makes it appear that we are on friendly terms with him."

Pain leaned back and closed his eyes in an effort to focus as he spoke. "One of the things Kip taught me about chess is that there is always one move that tips the entire game. Once that move is made, for all practical purposes, the match is essentially over. The trick is to avoid making that move."

Agony allowed herself a few moments to consider that and took another bite of her bagel before she spoke.

"I don't think we've made that move yet."

"Nor do I," he agreed. "As complicated and convoluted as our last couple of days have been, we have been very well-behaved pawns."

By now, she had grown tired of the chess references and was about to say so when a thought struck her. She didn't concern herself with trying to explain where it had come from. That would be too much at the moment.

Instead, she simply accepted it. Pain held onto chess moves as a way to help him keep his friend and partner Kip alive. She thought of her late partner and friend, All-in-Alex—Alejandro Infante—and his knitting while they were together on stakeouts and he worked on something for one of his children.

"Shit!" she had heard him mutter as he began to unravel the threads of the yarn he had concentrated on during the endless hours they had spent on that assignment when nothing was happening.

"Shit, what?" she'd asked him.

"Shit," he answered, "I missed a stitch."

"So back up a few stitches and start again." She hadn't understood at the time what the big deal was.

"I missed a stitch two days ago," he explained patiently and asked her to hold her hands out so he could rewind the yarn around them before he could pick up where he'd left off. "One wrong stitch is all it takes. No one else may know that you made it, but you will. It must be un-done. Otherwise, you will never be happy with the end result."

"We haven't missed a stitch yet," she exclaimed suddenly, and it was now Pain's turn to question his partner's sanity. "We merely don't know what pattern we should be working on."

Agony didn't wait for him to respond or to finish his bagel and barely gave him time to put the cup that held whatever was left of his coffee into its holder. She put Bertha into gear, chose a route toward the last place they had seen Agent Buchanan, and tried to explain as she drove.

"In a chess game..." She thought she might manage a proper analogy. "There are no do-overs, right?"

"That is how a game is played, yes." He wasn't sure where his partner was headed, either with Bertha or the conversation.

"In knitting, there are what we call unwinds." She had to be patient with both the traffic and her partner's comprehension. "You can unwind the whole work until you get to the stitch you dropped. If you catch that quickly enough, no one will ever know."

"We somehow missed a stitch with Buchanan." It wasn't a question.

"Maybe there's hope for you yet." She grinned at him. "We can't confront Buchanan in his fed-cave because that will give our dear landlady the impression that we are cooperating with him. But what we can do is stake out his professional lair and after he leaves it, we can follow him far away to where there are no prying eyes."

"Did I hear you correctly?" Pain wanted to make sure. "You want us to stalk a federal agent?"

"Exactly. He has to go home eventually—a place where we can all continue the conversations we had or didn't have, out of sight of any prying eyes or ears."

"And then..." He hoped he had understood her plan. "Then we can find a way to make everyone happy?"

"I don't think happy is in either Buchanan's or Ahjoomenoni's vocabulary," Agony answered as she guided Bertha to the street in front of Spook Central where they'd last encountered everyone's least favorite FBI agent, "but yeah. Something like that."

Pain let her drive in peace and decided to not badger her with questions until she'd parked.

"So the plan is?"

"We can't stake out the entire building," she replied. "If he drives himself and uses the parking garage then we, partner of mine, are shit out of luck. It'll be a long time before I go into another parking garage voluntarily."

"So," he asked as she put Bertha in park and they began their stakeout. "A lift-ride or a cab?"

"Neither." She was sure of that. "He is high enough on the fed food chain to be able to summon a driver when needed. I'd say he's the type to always be on duty and wants to be able to continue reviewing files without having to be bothered with chit-chat conversations with a driver while trying to get from point A to point B."

He could not think of any counter-argument and decided to simply hope she was right.

Fortunately, there was a fast-food chain half a block down that they used one at a time for bathroom breaks while they waited for Special Agent Marshal Buchanan. After three hours, their target finally appeared.

"Agent on the loose," Pain muttered and straightened in his seat.

Agony scanned the street and tried to locate a cab, a lift-ride, or an FBI black sedan to follow. After a quick stop at a street vendor's taco stand, Buchanan headed back inside.

If they'd had access to their P & A Investigation offices, they would have had computers that would have enabled them to trace everything there was to know about the agent. But they didn't so they couldn't and had to default to old-school.

All they could do was sit and wait. She retrieved her knitting supplies from the back of Bertha and he ran through the Sicilian Defense chess moves. He always did admire Bobby Fischer's aggressive play with the bishops.

Four hours later, Pain asked, "Other than the memory of your partner Alejandro, what is the attraction of knitting?"

"Idle hands are the devil's workshop?"

"I believe," he corrected, "that the quote is idle minds, not idle hands."

"And I believe you are correct." He suddenly felt a knitting needle about to be jammed into his ear. "But it's always good to have a needle ready to puncture a brain when too many stupid questions are asked."

Damn, she is as quick with her needles as she is with her guns.

A few more hours passed in relative silence and the sun had set before she put her needles down.

"What are we missing?" she asked.

"An agent." Pain thought the answer was obvious. "Damn, I wish we had access to our computers, or at least the DMV's computers to verify if he even has a car— Hey, how about your former sergeant? He's still on the force and was willing to help you before."

"Jeffries?" Agony shook her head. "That was on a missing minister case, not a we want to spy on a fed case. I won't drag him in on this one. No way."

"It was only a thought." He sighed. "If I had a make, model, and a license plate number at this point, I'd be willing to risk a trip to the parking garage."

"Whoa. We are getting desperate, aren't we?"

"What can I say?" He stepped out of Bertha and did some quick stretching. "Desperate times call for desperate measures."

Agony understood the need to stretch. At six-foot-four, he had five inches on her and even she was beginning to cramp up. As comfortable as the modified minivan was, they had been seated in it for over twelve hours.

"As far as we know," she said as she returned after a few stretches of her own, "he's been in there all day and now half the night. All we've done is watch for him. If he has been working all this time, I'd like to know what his secret energy drink is. Did we somehow manage to get old?"

"No, but we did manage to not burn ourselves out. He probably has a couch in his office. That is if he's even in his office and not at home enjoying a nightcap because he does drive himself. At this point, we know zilch."

"Deep throat!" She pulled her phone out.

"I'm afraid you lost me."

"You said parking garage. Woodward and Bernstein and Nixon and Deep Throat!"

"Lions and tigers and bears, oh my?" He held his hands up in surrender.

She dialed a number, put the phone on speaker as it rang, and held a finger up for silence. "Think Woodward and Bernstein...and..."

"Harry T, don't waste my time." Her favorite rabble-rousing reporter answered.

"It's time for me to call in that favor you owe me." She smiled.

"Do you know what time it is?" the reporter grouched.

"Yes, in fact, I do. It's time for you to return the favor of me tipping you off about the fireworks at the marina and the sinking of the Budria."

"Well," he admitted, "I did get considerable mileage out of that one. Wha'd'ya need, kiddo?"

"The make, model, license plate number, and home address of someone who may or may not have a car."

"Does this someone have a name?" Muffled noises in the background suggested that he'd retrieved his ever-present pen and notebook.

"Marshal Buchanan." She spelled both names for him.

"It doesn't ring a bell." They could hear the shrug in his voice. "Is this another missing minister, or have you and your behemoth of a partner slid into the spying on spouses business?"

"FBI Special Agent Marshal Buchanan," Pain interjected. He wasn't thrilled with the behemoth description but wasn't able to refute it either.

"A fed?" Harry Tribelescheau was suddenly more than casually interested.

"There's no story here yet, Harry." Agony wanted to make it clear. "And there may never be one. But you owe me."

"Stay tuned." He dropped the call.

"Sorry, partner." Agony leaned back and gave her eyes a brief rest. "I should have thought about Harry sooner."

"Better late than never." Pain accepted the apology. "At least you had someone to call."

There was a hint of sadness in his voice that she'd never heard before. It suddenly struck her that since losing his partner to the Treble Hook disaster, he had been cast adrift, anathema to his former employer and with no true support network to fall back on.

Ahjoomenoni and her Korean Mafia had treated him with respect, but there was no loyalty there as their current homeless situation testified to. He wore his lone-wolf persona so well that she had never considered what kind of emotional cost came with it. She didn't have time to delve too deeply into that revelation, however, because ten minutes later, Harry T had come through and her phone chirped with a text from a number she didn't recognize.

The message gave only a make, model, and plate number of a car, plus an address, and a *U-O-ME*.

"Harry T?" Pain looked hopeful.

"The man is good." She showed him the text, knowing he wouldn't need to write it down.

"An eight-year-old Camry." He didn't know what to make of that. "Comfortable, dependable, but not built for speed."

"Did you expect some kind of muscle car?" She didn't understand her partner's confusion. "Special Agent Buchanan didn't strike me as the type to pull up to a stoplight next to me and vroom-vroom his engine as if challenging me to a drag-race."

"I didn't expect anything. But now that I think about it, a mid-sized nondescript sedan does seem like his style. Give me ten."

Pain hurried across the street, moving quickly but not running until he slipped past the gates in the garage. He returned two minutes under his deadline.

"The car's there," he said as he scrambled in. "If he has a girlfriend, then all bets are off as to where he spends his nights. My money is still on a couch in his office. But at least we now know where he lives and I doubt that Ahjoomenoni has his home staked out. He'll have to go there eventually."

"It sounds like our safest bet to work out a deal without prying eyes and ears." Agony nodded. "I need one more quick potty break." She hurried to the fast-food franchise on the corner that had begun to seem like a second home, at least as far as bathroom amenities were concerned.

A few minutes later, she returned with a bag of burgers, fries, and two cups of lemonade. Stakeouts were hell on healthy eating but she didn't know what kind of access to food they would have while they waited for however long it would take the agent to return to his home sweet home.

Pain punched the address into Bertha's GPS and pulled the double CD of "Mad Dogs and Englishmen" from the glove box and slid in disc one. There was no way that his partner could fall asleep at the wheel while driving with that music playing.

Half an hour later, they were both surprised when they arrived at the address Harry T had given them. The Lake Wheeler Estates Apartments were nowhere near Lake Wheeler, which was located twenty miles outside of the city and was the center of high-end housing and apartment developments and a golf course.

One sight of the ten-unit apartment strip let everyone know that it had nothing to do with its namesake. If it resembled anything, it would be more of a one-story roadside motel with small apartments instead of motel rooms. Special Agent Buchanan occupied 1-H, the end unit.

"We now know two more things about him that we didn't know before," Pain commented as Agony guided Bertha into one of the three designated visitor parking spaces and he cut the CD off so Joe Cocker and Leon Russell & Company wouldn't disturb anyone's sleep.

"And those two things are?"

"He's not living high on the hog from taking bribes."

"And the second?" She agreed with his first assessment of Agent Buchanan's choice of abodes.

"He likes an easy commute to and from work. Even during rush hour, this is no more than a thirty-minute drive to or from his office."

"Can I offer a third observation?" she asked as she studied the surroundings. Even in the darkness, it was obvious that the Lake Wheeler Estates Apartments were surrounded by undeveloped land, half-woods and half-swamp.

"Please."

"He uses it as nothing more than a crash-pad. And," she added, "Unit 1-H is at the end. He likes his privacy."

"The more we learn about him," he admitted, "the more he's beginning to worry me."

"You and me both." She nodded. "I don't think you've made the one wrong move in one of your chess games yet..." She trailed off, not knowing what else to say.

"And I don't think you've missed a stitch." He appreciated her acknowledgment of his process and wanted to return the compliment to her in their analogies.

It was late at night and other than the blue glow from a couple of television screens or computers through the curtains, there wasn't any activity, interesting or otherwise.

After another half-hour of observation, Pain asked, "Do you think he has a woman waiting at home?"

"Maybe somewhere," she answered, "but that home isn't here. Shit, do you think he knows what we drive?"

"I wouldn't be surprised, but it's not like we can go get a rental. We'll have to take our chances."

"We can at least change our sign."

He nodded and rummaged in the back before he swapped the magnetic *Investigations* for *Animal Control* and made sure it covered the *P & A*. She waited while her partner walked nonchalantly to apartment 1-H. It took him thirty seconds to pick the lock and disable any burglar alarms before he waved her in.

Agony took the bag of burgers and fries and left the two lemonades behind as she hurried in to join him.

"We are now in the dragon's lair." She saved him the trouble of saying it himself as she closed the door behind her.

"Knit one, purl two." He smiled at her in the darkness and they settled in for the night.

CHAPTER EIGHT

They didn't turn any lights on or even use their phone's flashlight option to examine the apartment. You never knew when there would be prying eyes outside, maybe taking a dog out for a midnight piss or coming home late from a bar. With Lake Wheeler Estates Apartments being only a ten-unit building, the chances were good that the occupants all knew each other and their habits. Determined not to tip anyone off, they surveyed the agent's humble abode in the dark.

It wasn't exactly thrift-store quality furniture but wasn't anything to write home or brag about either. The small living room contained a sofa but no television. Beneath the window was a work desk with a comfortable chair, a lamp, and a laptop. The location of the desk allowed him to be able to look out the window. The whole set-up seemed designed to not allow anyone to come at him from behind.

A small kitchen held a table that could seat four but didn't leave much elbow room. The refrigerator contained no beer or wine and very little food, but it did have several small bottles of water and seltzer.

The bathroom had a shower but no tub. It seemed Agent

Buchanan wasn't the kind of man who would enjoy a long relaxing hot bath after a hard day at the office.

They moved into the bedroom. A double bed was neatly made up and the closet was full of FBI-approved suits, slacks, and shirts. There was also a reading lamp on the one nightstand next to the bed.

Few burgers or fries were left by the time the sun came up the next morning. They had rotated shifts to stretch on the sofa for a little shut-eye while the other sat at the desk, kept watch out the window, and wished they could risk turning the laptop on to do a little snooping. All in all, it was a thoroughly boring night, but at least they could stretch and use the bathroom without having to hike from Bertha to the corner.

Morning finally arrived but Buchanan still hadn't. They availed themselves of some bread and butter, both of which the agent kept in the fridge, and made themselves some toast. Enough light now came through the curtains to allow them to power the laptop up without giving themselves away, but it was seriously password protected and all they learned was that Buchanan's screensaver consisted of scrolling pictures of island beaches with crystal-clear water.

"Maybe," Pain suggested, "he simply sits here a lot and dreams of being on vacation."

"We could take his laptop to a hacker friend of mine."

He shook his head. "No, we need him more than we need to delve into his hard drive. Besides, this is a beauty and falls well above the lower limits of grand larceny. For all we know, it might also be government property and neither of us needs to have an arrest on our records."

"Would what we are now doing be considered breaking and entering?"

"Only if he presses charges. We'll have to convince him to not do that."

It was well into the afternoon when they heard a car pull up and park in front of the apartment. The partners sat side by side on the sofa. Their plan was to act like well-meaning intruders. They heard a car door open and close, followed shortly by the apartment door swinging open.

"I recognized the minivan. Do I need to come in with my guns drawn?" Buchanan called.

"If you do," Pain responded, "you'll have us at a disadvantage. We're not carrying."

"And if I don't believe you?"

"Then now would be a good time to call the cops. We'll wait."

After a brief pause, the agent entered carrying nothing but a briefcase that he placed on his desk. He looked at each of them in turn.

"Are you comfy?" he asked and slipped his suit jacket off and loosened his tie as he walked past them and into his bedroom. He returned a moment later, sat at his desk, and swiveled the chair so they could all face each other.

"I'll get you a gift card from IKEA for Christmas," Agony answered. "You could certainly do with some upgrades."

"Thank you for your generosity and critique."

"Seriously," she continued blithely, "do you think this is the kind of place any woman would want to be brought home to?"

"Only the kind of woman you find working the streets." Pain gave his opinion. "Or bring home in pieces in a couple of heavy-duty garbage bags."

"Wow." She frowned at her partner. "That went way darker than I expected."

"Look around," he explained. "I think the good agent is getting into method acting as a way to help track a serial killer. The clues are all here—end unit, woods and wetlands conveniently close, and a fridge and freezer practically empty, which is perfect for storing body parts ."

"Are you two almost done?" Buchanan demanded. "Your best bet is to draw the guns you claim not to be carrying and kill me now. Unless you plan to sit there and insult me to death?"

"I like the insulting to death option." Pain turned to his partner. "There wouldn't be much in the way of incriminating evidence left behind, right?"

"Right," she agreed. "I've never seen any charges brought against anyone for causing death by hurt feelings."

"I don't know what game you two are playing." The agent interrupted the not quite witty, in his opinion, repartee. "But you are dealing with a federal agent—"

"A federal *special* agent," Agony reminded him.

He shook the jibe off and in an effort to gain the upper hand, continued with his warning.

"You know the resources the FBI will throw into the arena when one of their own is the victim. You two will be in custody within two days and will never walk free in the sunlight again. Ever!"

"But that will be two days after the body is found," Pain retorted. "And between the woods and wetlands here, how long do you think it will take them to find your body? That is if we decide to dump it here and not load it in Bertha and take a cross-country tour. An arm in Ohio. A leg in Illinois. We'll save the head and hands for somewhere on the other side of the Mississippi. It would be a while before they can gather all the pieces, and by then—" He turned to his partner. "What are the countries that don't have any extradition agreements with the US?"

"It depends on which latitude or longitude we want to retire in," she responded after a moment's thought. "Fiji always sounded attractive."

"Seriously, bucko." He turned to their host again. "You don't know who you are fucking with if you think your FBI friends' limp-wristed investigations and manhunts make us sweat."

"You're assuming he has any friends," she pointed out to her partner and turned to Buchanan. "You are the one who inserted himself into our business, which makes me cranky. So please, when we come to you in the spirit of friendship, please, please and double-please, don't give me another reason to want to have to scrape you off the bottom of these tastefully casual shoes."

"No," the agent answered, "none of us want to pursue anything that would lead to that scenario." He sensed that the immediate threat of danger had passed and that they might be there to play ball. All he had to do was determine what their game was.

"Do you mind if I get some water?" he asked as he stood and headed to his fridge without waiting for an answer. He unscrewed the cap and returned to his chair, drinking directly from the bottle to save him having to do any more dishes than necessary.

"What?" Pain asked. "You're not going to offer us any?"

"I'm very sure you know where it is and are thoroughly capable of helping yourselves."

"Well, yeah, that's true," he acknowledged and added, "By the way, you are now down two slices of bread and a pat or two of butter."

"I'll manage to survive the devastation somehow. So, who goes first?"

"On the level?" Agony had difficulty trusting him, but they had stalked him for the express purpose of having a productive conversation, so she tried hard to give the fed-snake the benefit of the doubt.

"On the level," he replied. "You want something from me. If it's access to any ongoing investigations, you may as well escort yourselves out the door because that won't ever happen."

"All we want," Pain stated, "is to put you in our rearview mirror and we are wondering what kind of costs will come with that."

"Are you offering a bribe to a federal agent?" Buchanan gave them another of his smiles that fell far short of reaching his eyes. "Do you know how serious that is?"

Pain was pissed. He'd thought they'd been making some progress. "Are you seriously that—" He paused when he noticed the smile, which he didn't like at all.

"Were you born with instantly irritating in your DNA, Agent Buchanan?" Agony didn't like the smile any more than her partner did. "Or is it something you had to take extra classes to perfect?"

"*Special* Agent Buchanan," he reminded her as she had reminded him earlier, his ice-smile still in place.

She came to the conclusion that she could spend the rest of her life never hearing the word "special" again and die a happy woman.

"The woodlands and the wetlands." Pain had a growl in his voice. "And a cross-country body-part-disposal trip sounds increasingly appealing. Will you cut to the chase anytime soon, or do we have to see how much damage your garbage disposal can do?"

"Yeah, the disposal works well." To his credit, Buchanan remained fairly nonchalant about the threat to his body parts. "It's not as fast or effective as a wood-chipper in North Dakota, but it could certainly do some damage until the bones started clogging it up."

"We're waiting." Agony was becoming impatient and her response confirmed for Pain that she wasn't much of a movie-watching gal because she had missed the wood-chipper reference completely.

"Ahjoomenoni." The only surprise about the agent's one-word answer was that he'd voiced it so soon.

"That is not an option." Pain shut that line of negotiations down quickly. "She is out of the equation."

"She has a long history." The agent tried to push again. "Foreign intelligence, drug running, and God only knows what else." He focused his attention on him. "And she seems to be a friend of yours, which puts you in a very exposed position, my friend."

"I've had worse friends." Pain's look made certain that the agent understood that he was one of them.

"I haven't," Agony interjected, "but the salty old bitch is my landlady so I'm willing to make an exception and accept her, warts and all. So if that's all you have, we are done here, don't'cha know, eh?"

Whoa, Pain thought, *she isn't as hopeless as she seems.*

The agent leaned back and threw his hands up in surrender. "No Ahjoomenoni. I get it. She scares me too, which is why the only thing I've ever done to her is skirt around the edges. I merely want to keep reminding her that she's not free and clear to do anything she wants."

"Well, there's the crux of the matter." Pain saw no point in delaying. "She wants you out of her life and we want you out of ours. Both goals are intertwined. You must have something else to offer."

"Can I take a leak first?" Buchanan asked. "It's hard for me to think when a full bladder is calling."

"The bathroom's straight down the hallway." Pain shrugged to indicate permission.

"Yeah, I know." The agent stood. "I've been here before."

"We still don't know what the game is," Agony whispered once she heard the bathroom door close.

"I have a feeling we're about to find out," he responded. "He's about to make a move."

"Same vibe here," she said as they heard the toilet flush and hands being washed a moment later. Special Agent Marshal Buchanan returned to his seat, looking physically relieved but mentally uneasy. A very long moment of silence followed while the partners waited for him to commit himself.

"Look..." Buchanan leaned forward and stared at the nondescript carpet, "I don't expect your help on this but I have another op."

"An op that's more important than Ahjoomenoni?" Pain asked skeptically.

"Ahjoomenoni is more of a hobby than an op." The agent raised his head and faced them. "At this point, she's probably become more a habit than a hobby. Everything there is merely surface scratching, and I know I'll never get beneath it. But there is something else—a much more localized situation where I might be able to make a difference if I could only get my higher-ups interested in it."

"We're listening," Pain replied encouragingly. He sensed that the real game was now on and the only question was whether or not he and Agony would simply be pawns in it.

"It involves a deep-cover investigation into some very influential but probably corrupt political civil service figures. My higher-ups refuse to pay any attention to it." He leaned back and sighed. "They think I'm on a fishing expedition. Have you ever experienced something like that?"

The partners nodded. They had.

"But you know it." He was beginning to sound sincerely passionate and not simply annoyingly snarky. "You just know it. You wonder why it looks like I barely live here? It's because I have spent all my free time digging into it. Powerful people making dirty back-room deals far from the public eye."

"How powerful and how dirty?" It was Agony's turn to ask and he leaned forward to be able to look her straight in the eye as he answered.

"There is a former female detective who was once a rising star on the city's police force, who now has a contract out on her placed there by people unknown."

That statement took his partner so much by surprise that Pain felt obliged to ask. "Proof?"

"None," The agent shook his head.

"Suspicion level?"

"High."

"Bullshit level?"

"None. Look, I don't know if these people were responsible for the contract," Buchanan admitted, "but they are in the position to be able to do it. Like I said, I can't get permission to launch a full-scale op but I do have access to a discretionary fund to use, within limits. But those limits will be enough to support two operatives for a few days to infiltrate, gather as much information as possible, and report back. The only action you two would need to do is stretch your acting muscles for a few days. Do you think you might be up for something like that?"

"And the contract out for me," Agony asked, "might or might not be involved?"

"I have no way of knowing at this point," the agent admitted, "but everyone with their ear to the ground knows it's out there. Maybe it was a low blow on my part to use it to draw you in"—it was almost an apology—"but these are the types to be able to pull it off."

"The whole Ahjoomenoni thing was nothing more than a ruse to draw us in, wasn't it?" Pain was not at all happy about having been used as pawns thus far.

"Yes," the man conceded. "Guilty as charged."

"And it left us homeless and officeless." He was truly pissed. "And with no choice but to track you down and play nice."

"Which you did." Buchanan nodded. "And which you are now doing. Look, you two can walk out of here right now and I will agree to leave Ahjoomenoni alone for a year out of courtesy for you hearing me out. But if you walk out, you will never know how much good you could have done."

"Or how many feathers we could help put in your federal cap after your big score." Agony shared her partner's anger at having been used.

"Look around." The agent spread his arms. "Does it look like

I'm someone who is interested in big scores? Working for justice is my whole reason for existence. You can either buy that or not. But now is the time to decide."

"A moment, please?" Pain asked as he stood and gestured for his partner to join him outside for a quick consultation.

"The door is unlocked." Buchanan motioned toward it. "Take your time. This is a serious decision and I don't want you to have to rush. At the same time, I need to get some sleep so please decide soon."

The partners stepped outside.

CHAPTER NINE

"How far do you trust him?" Agony asked as they walked a short distance into the graveled parking lot.

Pain spat in his right hand, slapped it together with his left, and pulled them apart slowly. The spittle stretched for all of one inch before it separated.

"Crude," she said, "but very effective as a visual aid."

"All right, then. Let's simplify. Who do you trust?"

"No one." In her mind, this was the only possible answer.

"Oh." He sighed as he raised his hands to his chest and placed them over his heart. "I am deeply hurt."

"Then maybe you phrased the question wrong," she informed the current reigning parking-lot drama queen. "Do you care to try again?"

"Other than ourselves," he rephrased, "who can we trust?"

"No one." Her answer remained the same.

"Well, at least we're on the same page there," he answered and began to walk in a slow circle.

She had learned that once a plan was decided upon and put into place, he could sit as still as the subjects in a portrait painting as they worked through their next moves. It was only during the decision-making process that he seemed to have the need to keep his feet in motion.

"Priorities?" he asked as he circled her slowly. She had also learned to not try to spin inside her partner's circles and follow him with her eyes as he paced. It could lead to a serious case of vertigo. She kept her eyes fixed on the agent's door as she answered.

"Find a place to live." She began to list them in order. "Get back to our office and continue with our efforts to earn a low-paying but mostly honest living."

"And for that to happen," he agreed, "we need to get back into Ahjoomenoni's good graces."

She considered the options for a moment. "Either that or change our names, move out of the state or country, and try our hands at running a llama ranch."

"Llamas can spit as far as camels." He spoke as if from personal experience.

"I'll trust you on that and I agree, Ahjoomenoni should be our priority. So, do we take Buchanan out now or play along? I'm good either way."

"I think we need to play along." Pain stopped his pacing, having reached his conclusion. "Ahjoomenoni is our priority but Buchanan is the one who holds the key."

Agony didn't argue with her partner's reasoning. "My main concern right now is what door does the key unlock, and what kind of mayhem will be waiting for us inside the room?"

"There's only one way to find out. Do we head for spitting llama country or slimy the slimy fed?"

"The fed is much closer and I don't know one damn thing about llamas."

Their decision reached, they returned to Buchanan's door and were polite enough to knock before they entered.

Special Agent Marshal Buchanan opened the door and gave them what passed, for him, as a genial smile as he waved them in. The smile put both the partners on high alert.

"The door was unlocked," he reminded them.

"Sometimes," Pain answered as he followed his partner in, "we prefer to err on the side of politeness."

"That's commendable." The agent nodded and dropped his attempt at a friendly smile because he knew it wasn't something that looked very natural for him. "Please, we need to go to the kitchen table but don't worry about taking a seat. You will want to be standing for this."

They moved to the small kitchen where the table had been cleared of any plates or silverware. All it held was a thick sheaf of papers that covered one half, leaving the other half of the surface free for the agent to lay his collection out one sheet at a time.

"You were right," Buchanan admitted. "I used your relationship with Ahjoomenoni to draw you in. And you have to admit that it was effective."

That didn't come as a surprise to them. What did come as a surprise was when he looked at them over the table and, with a slight change of voice, said, "I love it when a plan comes together."

Pain turned to his partner and spoke loudly enough for everyone in the room to hear. "Did he try to pull a Hannibal Smith impersonation on us?"

"I think so," she replied, "but the intonation was all wrong and I don't see a cigar in sight. He needs to work on that."

"Do you think we've both been played?"

Agony put the back of her hand to her forehead and tried her impersonation, this one of Scarlett O'Hara. "Oh, dear. Hustled by a federal agent with a convoluted haircut and a horrid talent for impersonations. However shall I live this down?"

She spun and fainted backward into Pain's arms. He was

tempted to let her fall but being the good partner that he was, he caught her and helped her to her feet.

"At this point," Pain informed them, "I'm not sure what to do other than let both of you live long enough to be able to go over whatever the plans are and then, before we go our separate ways, kill the first one who holds their hand up in a weird-ass salute and says, 'Live long and prosper.'" He tried his impersonation of a prison warden from one of his favorite films. "Am I being clear enough for you, or am I being too obtuse?"

Then, for good measure and because he was on a roll, he threw in another prison warden impression from a much earlier film. "What we are dealing with here is a failure to communicate." *Damn, I love Newman's performance as Cool Hand Luke.*

"Here is what I have." Agent Buchanan left the fun of the dramatic performances and critiques behind as he drew their attention to the table and the layers of papers he was ready to spread out and show them one at a time as he tried to focus their interest.

"This is called the Moorfin Lodge," he said as he slid the first photograph out for them to look at. It was a wide aerial view of a large complex surrounded by woodlands and nowhere near the city.

"I've never heard of it," Pain said as he studied the image.

"Very few have," Buchanan confirmed, "and that is by intentional design. The Moorfin and its owners and members want to stay as far away from prying eyes as possible. Camp David's location in Maryland is not on any public map, although the restricted airspace within a two-hundred-mile radius of it does provide a clue to its location."

He continued. "The Moorfin Lodge's location is almost as hard to narrow down. Not because of any government security issues but because that's the way they want it. Prying eyes are not appreciated."

"Why?" Pain asked. "Too many coke-head public figures running around naked and having orgies at the poolside?"

The agent chuckled. "Something like that."

"We don't care about something like." Agony scrutinized the photo that was spread on the free-half of the table and frowned. "We only care what it is exactly like."

"We're leveling with each other here, right?" Buchanan asked.

"That would be a first." Agony was ready to put a bullet through his head and start studying llama ranching.

"The Moorfin Lodge," the agent continued without taking offense, "is a whispered secret. You have to be either very rich, very powerful in a political sense, or both to even know of its existence. It is not a celebrity retreat or rehab center where paparazzi wait outside to snatch a pic of whatever latest A-list actor or actress or has-been-child-star has checked into for rehab. If there is an action movie star who has recently exited his closet and is looking for social media support for the happy couple, the Moorfin isn't the place for them either. "

"So," she asked, "if I were a Hollywood starlet who had hooked up with her married co-star in the latest blockbuster movie, you're telling us that the Moorfin might not be the best place to chill out?"

"You wouldn't even be let in the gate." The agent nodded, glad that at least one of them had paid attention to him. "The members are the type of powerful people who don't want any attention drawn to them, which makes them the most dangerous of breeds. Everyone there is a bird of prey, and I apologize in advance for not being able to come up with a more original quote but birds of a feather flock together."

"And exactly what do these birds do when they flock?" Pain finally joined the conversation again.

"Whatever kind of carnage they wish," Buchanan told him with a sad shake of his head. "All kinds of dealings, some simply nefarious, some utterly evil, and all done far away from the public eye. I have, on my own time, started a"—he looked at the ex-agent before he continued—"let's call it a quest." His use of the word sent a chill down Pain's spine. "I have gathered many pieces of the puzzle. I merely don't have enough information yet to put the pieces together."

"And that's where we come in?" he asked.

Buchanan knew about the hit put out on Agony. His dropping "quest" in also let the partners know that he had done his homework on Pain's humble self. That told them that the agent was playing a long-run, long-shot game and was either using them or needed them in order to be able to keep playing.

"Show us what else you have," Pain requested after Agony gave him a nod.

Buchanan pulled out sheet after sheet of aerial photographs, all of them personally annotated with notes in permanent ink markers in various colors, ranging from red to yellow to green to blue, with a few circles thrown in for clarification's sake.

"There's a great deal of territory to cover," Pain commented.

"I prefer overkill to under-informed." The agent did not apologize. "If you two are willing to take this on, you will need to know everything you can about the lay of the land. This should be an easy-in, easy-out assignment to observe and then report. But if you two somehow manage to fuck up, you both need to know that you are on your own with no backup."

"In other words…" He needed to hear the agent say it. "This is a personal, strictly off the books op?"

"That is exactly what it is," Buchanan confirmed. "I'm willing to burn a year's worth of my FBI discretionary funds to finance this for a few days."

"But no funds from your pocket?" Agony thought it was a fair question to ask.

"If two or three days isn't enough time for you two to be able to give me what I need," he answered, "then no one has deep enough pockets to be able to continue. These are bad people doing bad things."

"How bad?" Pain asked as he flipped through the aerial photos.

"How bad what? The people or the things?" Buchanan asked in return.

"And who are the people?" Agony voiced her question before her partner could speak.

"At this point, I have more questions than answers." Buchanan tried to address both of them at once. "So I honestly don't know."

"Yeah, we heard you the first time." Pain tried a quick follow-up question, "Do the bad things involve goat sacrifices? Because if so, I'm all in on trying to stop them. Goats are fun little critters."

"Really?" Agony wasn't sure if her partner was being sincere or mocking.

"Really," he replied. "I once spent three months on an op hiding out on a goatherder's farm and became friendly enough with some of the goats to give them names. My favorite was the one I christened Casper."

"Casper?"

She fell for it and then realized her mistake when Pain replied, "The friendly goat."

"Please, dear God," she muttered and rolled her eyes heavenward, "take one of us now before I break whatever commandment that says 'Thou shalt not kill.'"

"You two should take your comedy act on the road." Buchanan decided it was time to end the comedy part of the conversation. "Because I'm sure that somewhere between the Poconos and Poughkeepsie, dozens of lounges would be willing to sign you up for at least a two-night stand."

"My bad." Pain raised his hands in apology.

"Do you at least know who our targets are?" Agony brought the discussion back to the realm of reality.

"I honestly don't know." The agent followed her serious question with a serious answer. "In the surveillance I was able to get before I was shut down, I couldn't nail down exactly who the ringleader was. So no." He turned to Pain. "I don't know the level of animal sacrifices or what kind of livestock was involved."

Her partner had a faraway look in his eyes so she continued. "What I hear from you, Special Agent Buchanan, is that the vice president could arrive to offer human sacrifices to the One-Eyed, Seven Prick Star-Fuckers, but that might not be what we should keep an eye out for?"

"Bingo!" the agent replied, an exclamation that only elicited a couple of groans. "Although I'm very sure that the vice president will be out of the country on a fruitless diplomatic mission while you are there. But hey, maybe the Speaker of the House or a television rating's king of a televangelist will show up. Who knows?"

"Thanks for the offer." Pain returned from wherever his mind had taken him. "But I think we'll pass."

"Oh, come on, man," Buchanan started before he cut him off.

"Don't come on man me, bro. I smell someone who's in over his head here and is looking for a couple of fools to bail him out. I'm gone."

He moved toward the door but stopped when the other man said, "I don't need fools! I need a couple of hard-asses who aren't afraid of a group of middle-aged folks hanging out and trying to catch a tan, and maybe sneak in an affair or two on the side. But I guess I misjudged you two."

"You didn't misjudge anything." Pain returned to the table. "Except the susceptibility of a couple of professionals to be conned."

"I'm not running a con here!" Buchanan somehow managed to sound sincere again. "There is something there. I know there is, and I know that you two can understand that feeling. Or maybe I misjudged you. You know the way to the door."

He started restacking his pile of photos and made one last

attempt. "Bad people doing very bad things. From what I know about you two, I thought you would give a damn."

"Hold on, Pain." Agony turned back from the door. "You do realize that if we find out you've merely been stringing us along, it will not end happily for you."

Buchanan nodded. "If I have been, as you say, merely stringing you along, I am well aware that I will have to spend the rest of my nights sleeping with one eye open. So yes, I understand. But ever since I stumbled onto the Moorfin Lodge and what I suspect is going on there, I haven't slept very well at all, so I'm not worried about losing any shut-eye. But if I'm right and you two are as good as I think you are, I might be able to get a good night's sleep when all is said and done."

"I'll trust your instincts on this one, Agony." Pain still had his doubts about the man but none about his partner.

She took a step into the room. "If we sign on for you completely off the books, then whether we get what you're hoping for or whether the whole thing ends up with you jousting at windmills, you'll get off Ahjoomenoni's back?"

"Ahjoomenoni who?" The agent gave her a version of a smile that almost reached his eyes. "If I'm wrong, then I'm wrong, but I don't think I am. They're up to something, I'm sure of that, but I need your help to find out what it is."

Agony was almost ready to accept. "And if you're right and we manage to gather the intel you're hoping for, what can you do with it? The whole op is unauthorized."

"Completely unauthorized." The agent was glad that everyone in the room understood that very important point. "But my gut tells me something seriously wrong is going on there. In spite of all of my FBI training, every now and then, I need to trust my gut. I want to follow it but I need a direction in which to aim it."

"Partner?" she asked while still looking at the agent.

"It's your call. Right or wrong, I'll back your play."

"So, Special Agent Marshal Buchanan—"

"Excuse me," Pain interjected and addressed the other man. "Have you ever considered leaving the FBI and signing up with the US Marshalls? That way you could be called Marshall Marshal."

Pain didn't know if it was the interruption or the play on words. What he did learn though, was that Agony could throw a mean elbow to the ribs.

"What can I say?" She apologized. "I found him as a stray on the street and tried to leave him at the pound. They wouldn't take him and I've been stuck with him ever since. I almost have him house-broken now, though, so maybe you want him?"

"Sorry." Buchanan shook his head. "The apartments have a very strict no-pets policy."

"Pity." She shook her head. "So, as I started to say, if the Moorfin Lodge is so exclusive, how do you plan to get us in there? Unlike the overgrown puppy here, I'm not trained in midnight parachute drops."

"Aahhh," the agent answered. "This is the fun part."

CHAPTER TEN

"You forgot to mention there was a fun part." Pain was still only half-sold on the scheme but he closed the door. "You"—he pointed at the agent—"chair. Us? We'll take the sofa."

"Me, Jane," Agony responded without a trace of humor. "You Tarzan."

"You," he informed the agent, "Cheeta."

"Is Cheeta allowed to order a pizza?" the agent asked and took the instructions without rancor as he settled into his desk chair that he knew was far more comfortable than the sofa. He swiveled to face them.

"That up to Jane." Pain grunted.

"Oh, for mercy's sake." She sat on one end of the sofa. "If we're going to be here that long, order a damn pizza."

"Toppings?" Buchanan asked before he added, "And yes, we may be here for a while."

"I know the best way to decide on pizza toppings when more than one person is involved." Pain sat on the sofa as far away from his partner that he could manage since she didn't seem particularly pleased with him at the moment. "It's for everyone to state clearly what they do not want on it. Then, whatever's left is what we order."

After several minutes of debate, they settled on onions, tomatoes, and Italian sausage.

"Huh, how about that?" Buchanan looked up from the notes he'd been taking. "We may as well order some calzones."

"Order the damn pizza and be done with it!" Pain tended to get grumpy when he was tired and hungry and wanted to get into the details of an op.

The agent placed the order for delivery and relaxed into his chair. He studied the partners he had drawn in and who currently sat as far away from each other as his sofa allowed.

"Have you two ever considered taking out a restraining order on each other?"

"It's crossed my mind a time or two," Agony admitted.

"I'm waiting for the judge's decree to arrive at any minute," Pain retorted, "but it will be delivered to an address we no longer have access to, Special Agent Buchanan. So how about you get on with it?"

He was able to reassure them. "First of all, you two won't need to do much acting."

"And why is that?" Agony felt it was her responsibility to ask since she had made the call to bring her and her partner into whatever Buchanan had in mind and Pain remained as far away from her as possible without sitting on the sofa's arm.

"Because," the agent informed them, "you will go as an uber-rich married couple who are currently having a hard time to even be in the same room with each other."

"So," Pain queried, "no method acting needed?"

"Not as far as I can see." Buchanan, for once, was able to be completely honest with the two of them.

"I like the premise so far," Agony answered the agent as she gave her partner a side-eyed look that seemed to threaten to turn his body into stone if he spoke again anytime soon. "Tell us—or at least me—more."

Pain took the hint, closed his eyes, and envisioned Bishop to Queen's four, a very effective defensive move that Kip would have been proud of him for having remembered. He'd learned it when they'd been in the middle of a mental match and were fifty hours into a specific op. He couldn't even remember what country they had been in at the time, but he remembered Kip's smile when he made his move. It ended up being one of the four matches out of the hundreds they had played that he had won.

Kip had drilled it into his head. "If you lose the queen, your best option is to fake an enormous sneeze and use whatever body parts that are convenient to accidentally upend the whole board and send it tumbling to the floor because you will most likely be toast."

Protect the pain in the ass queen at all costs, he thought and did his best to bite his tongue as Agony continued with the negotiations and details of the assignment that was currently being explained by their new best friend—friend being a relative term.

"It was almost a year ago." He tuned into the conversation in time to hear Buchanan respond to what must have been a question his partner had posed. "There was another agent. Her first name was, and still is, Veronica. Ronnie is what she goes by. We planned to go to Moorfin together as a dysfunctional couple."

"What happened?" Agony asked and Pain wished he had some popcorn. Fortunately, he remembered that a pizza was on its way.

"Red tape is what happened," Special Agent Buchanan answered. "I had the identities all lined up. I would go as an up-and-coming property management mogul who had scraped together enough power, prestige, money, and a reputation for skirting around the edges of the law in a bend-don't-break kind of way. He would feel completely at home amongst the other guests at the Moorfin."

"And Ronnie?" she asked since she had the feeling that the woman's role was the one she would have to play.

"Ronnie was going to play the asshole mogul's wife. An heiress to part of a small fortune who, with the assistance of a very high-powered attorney, managed to cut both ex-wives and her siblings out of any rights to the estate days before their old man passed away of a heart attack."

"She sounds like a ruthless bitch to me." Pain looked at his partner and smiled. "I think you'll be able to pull it off."

"Oh, yeah, Mr. Mogul." She smiled in return. "Like you're any great catch yourself."

Agent Buchanan watched as the partners dropped their defensive postures and began to get settled into their assigned personas. Not that it would be too hard to do.

"What happened to Ronnie?" Agony beat Pain to the question.

The agent sighed regretfully. "The silly girl had the audacity to fall in love and left the bureau."

"She became a soccer mom?" Pain thought it was a logical assumption.

"No." The other man shook his head sadly and answered, "That, I could have made a reasonable argument against. He was a jazz-style drummer, which I have learned is a very specific art. If you want to try to track her down, your best bet is on a cruise ship. The last I heard from her, she was learning how to sing some scat somewhere on a liner in the Caribbean area. Her man and his band are already booked for the next three years on the Cruise Line Circuit."

"So…" Agony continued her line of questioning. She had already had enough scat for one day. "I am an heiress not quite happily married to my limp-weed mogul of a spouse. All we have to do is show up as an overly rich, imbecilic idiot couple with no morals, who will tickle the fancy of the actual players at the Moorfin. They will be glad to draw them in and suck them dry?"

"That about sums it up, yeah," Buchanan answered as he

walked to the door, accepted the pizza that was delivered right on time, and gave the driver a decent tip before he placed the box on the small kitchen table.

"Is anyone else hungry," he asked, "or shall I be dining alone?"

"I could go for a slice." Pain sighed and left his seat to follow the aroma to the small table.

"A slice of what?" Agony made a stab for one of his sleeves to slow his momentum. "A slice of pizza or a slice of Buchanan's neck?"

"Either or." He gave her a smile that told her he was almost sold. "At this point, I'm not fussy."

The agent spoke after he'd finished his first slice. "It will take me most of tomorrow to get the identity cards changed to match your physical appearances."

"We've never eaten pizza together before," Agony commented as she made short work of her first slice.

"Are you sure?" Pain searched his memory banks.

"I would have remembered. You're one of those."

"One of what?" He frowned at her.

"A pizza two-fer."

"Oh." He looked at the two slices he was eating at the same time by placing one slice face down on the other sandwich-style. "I didn't know there was a name for it."

"Well, there is," she insisted, "and I can confirm that it looks a little piggish."

Pain shrugged. "It's a habit. I don't always have time to relax through a leisurely meal. I consider it a time-saver and it has often come in handy."

She shook her head since there was no point in arguing with a barbarian. Turning back to Buchanan, she picked up the conversation.

"These new identity cards…I assume driver's license and things like that. Will we have to pose for headshots?"

"There's no need. I already have enough footage on you two to be able to pull the pics I need."

That statement didn't make either of the partners comfortable but they weren't surprised.

By this point, Pain was becoming convinced that this had been the agent's plan all along. It wasn't only Ahjoomenoni he wanted. It was them and the new identity cards had probably already been created. The "I'll need a day" comment was simply a way for him to sound as if he was winging it. His suspicion seemed to be confirmed when the agent spoke again.

"You two will have to look the part, so I have arranged a special-fitting session at the Syeni Boutique. You'll need an assortment of wardrobes. For undergarments, you'll be on your own, but outerwear will need to be appropriate for the location. And don't get too comfortable because everything will be rented for the occasion and will have to be returned when the mission is over."

"So, no spilling red wine on my nice white gown?" Pain asked.

"I believe that should be my line." Agony was tired of shaking her head at his idiocy. "Are you sure your apartment has a no-pets policy?"

"Very sure," Buchanan informed her. "Besides," he added as Pain bit into his second pizza two-fer, "I couldn't afford to feed him."

"I had to ask." She sighed. "But I also have to ask—although it isn't a question when I already know the answer. You planned all of this from the beginning simply to rope us in, didn't you?"

Buchanan screwed his face into a satisfied grin and looked around for something to use as a prop-cigar, clearly about to do another of his Hannibal Smith impressions before she cut him off.

"Pain? What would you say to someone who's about to do a bad Hannibal impression for the second time in one night?"

Pain swallowed the bite he was chewing, cleared his throat, and did a very impressive Mr. T. "I pity the fool."

The partners turned down the offer to order dessert and having been given all the information they needed, they wished the agent a not completely genial good night and left. They had a big day of shopping ahead.

"Why do I feel like I need a shower?" Pain asked as Agony headed toward a nearby inexpensive motel where they could afford a couple of single rooms out of their petty cash fund.

"I don't know if I need an entire shower," she answered, "but I would certainly like to be able to hose off from the knees down. There was a huge pile of bullshit to wade through in there."

They reached the one-story, two-wing motel and walked into the shabby office, arriving half an hour before the desk clerk would display the No Vacancy sign and head to bed.

"Two single rooms, please," Pain asked as the short, thin man welcomed them.

"Two rooms?" The clerk didn't want to pry but he was curious as to why the couple didn't want one double room. It would have saved them money.

"Two rooms," he repeated. "One for us and one for our...um, goats."

"Two rooms please." Agony was tired. "I need some alone time."

"I understand." He didn't press the odd couple any further and assigned them the only two single rooms that were still available, one in each wing.

They gathered what they needed from Bertha and walked to the corner where the wings separated.

"Mañana?" Pain asked to keep up the tradition.

"Mañana," she answered. Both of them were tired and needed to work through some thoughts on their own before they regrouped the following day.

The morning dawned bright and clear. Their appointment at the Syeni was at 10:00 am and after a quick stop for donuts and coffee, they arrived half an hour early. They had four hours to get their outfits together before Buchanan would have a limo driver with their new IDs in an envelope pick them up for the two-hour drive to the Moorfin.

They found a parking garage where they could leave Bertha and gathered a few essentials and two large, empty suitcases. The luggage was nowhere near top of the line and wouldn't impress anyone at the Moorfin, but they were better than large garbage bags and they had to have something to pack their upcoming rental clothing in.

The owner of Syeni greeted them, suitcases and all, as they walked into her very spacious boutique. In her well-preserved early-fifties, she almost matched Agony in height until you threw in the five-inch stilettos that gave her a three-inch advantage.

"You must be Richard and Sheri, arriving fashionably early." She wasn't overly pleased with their early arrival but shook their hands. "I am Andrea. I am afraid it will be a few minutes before your assistants are ready, and wine while waiting isn't allowed before noon. But we have several beverages on the table for you to help yourselves to while you wait. It won't be for very long. The twins are eager to get started."

"We have managed over the last couple of decades," Agony informed her, "to learn how to choose clothes for ourselves."

"Of course you have, dear." Andrea gave one of her cheeks an understanding pat. "But I was told that this is a special occasion and as such, we must all sometimes call upon professionals. Think of it this way—if you had a slight cut on your arm, you would know how to put some ointment and a band-aid on it. But if you were to unfortunately break an arm…well, certainly, you would seek out a proper doctor, correct?"

"Well, yeah," she admitted but wasn't sure that selecting a few outfits would be cause enough to have to visit an emergency room.

"Trust me on this." The owner patted her other cheek and took hold of her chin gently to turn her face left and right. "You have wonderful skin tone. The twins will have an easy time with you. As for your beau..." She stepped back and studied Pain. "Well, we'll see what we can do to make him as presentable as possible. He has a nice frame, though, so that is a good canvas to work with. I'll check on the twins and see how they are coming along. They are my two best associates and are excited by the challenge."

She left them alone and strode elegantly toward the back room.

"If she touches me one more time, I may have to pull my baton out and show her what a broken arm feels like."

"If she refers to me as your beau again, you will have my complete support to baton away."

The partners helped themselves to a couple of small bottles of room temperature seltzer. They had begun to wander around and look through the racks when Andrea returned with the twins in tow. The partners would be treated to a brother-sister act.

"This is Jean." The owner introduced the sister, who smiled politely. "And this is Gino." He also smiled and both had a gleam in their eyes as they surveyed the couple.

"I want the big guy," Jean whispered into her brother's ear.

"Oh, sister of mine," he responded, "who wouldn't?"

The twins shared wonderful genes and posture—perfect cheekbones, striking amber-colored eyes, and wavy brown hair cut in almost identical styles that reached almost to their shoulders. The hairstyle managed to look good on both of them.

Jean smiled as she took Pain's elbow and Gino wore the same as he took Agony's and they led them to the back where one of the dressing room-critiquing areas was located. There were two dressing rooms with three comfortable chairs in the common room.

"Please now, my dear. Relieve your feet and have a seat," Gino said as he guided her to a chair. Jean did the same with Pain. Once seated, the twins stepped back and ran through their assignment.

"We have been informed," the brother began, "that we will need three outfits for dinner and evening affairs, along with three afternoon soirees of varying degrees of casual."

"And," his sister added, "three sets of appropriate lounging around clothing for the mornings and between activities. Does that sound about right for your adventure?"

"If you say so." Pain shrugged.

"Oh, we do." Gino tsked. "Don't go anywhere, now. We'll be back in as quick of a jiff as we can."

With that, the twins hurried away on their expedition.

"Buchanan doesn't even trust us to be able to choose our own clothes?" Pain ventured.

"No more than we trust him to have been completely on the up and up with us."

"Which is not much." He sipped his seltzer and continued. "Much of this seems a little sloppy and not well thought out, and that doesn't seem like him. He spent considerable time and effort to reel us in, only to send us off like a couple of half-cocked pistols without a specific target. What's wrong with this picture?"

Agony didn't have time to answer as the twins returned, holding up a set of matching evening wear.

"Oh." She didn't give them a chance to say anything. "No, no, no, and no. The last thing we want to do is dress like a couple of —" She almost said twins but caught herself in time. "Matching bookends. Pretend we don't like each other but need to keep up appearances. We both need to look good but each in our separate way."

"But these would be perfect together." Gino pouted.

"Yes, they would," Agony tried to assuage their hurt feelings. "But we don't want to look perfect together. We want to make the other one cry with how good we can both look when we are not standing arm in arm pretending to be the perfect couple."

"Well..." Jean sniffed. "If that's the way you want it."

"Such a delightful couple," Gino whispered to his sister but loudly enough for their clients to hear as they hurried onto the floor. It did not sound like a compliment.

"Three and a half more hours of this?" Agony sighed.

"It's only two hundred and ten more minutes." Pain tried to put it into a different perspective. "Or twelve thousand and six hundred seconds if that makes it any easier for you to handle."

"One Mississippi. Two Mississippi. Three Mississippi." Agony started counting. Two hundred and forty Mississippis later, he realized that she wasn't bluffing. She intended to keep counting. He started singing "Ninety-nine bottles of beer on the wall" softly.

She was up to four-hundred and ninety Mississipis and he was down to sixty-two bottles when the twins rolled in a hanger cart full of men's attire.

"We decided," Gino informed Agony, "that we will go with a different strategy. First, we shall try our best to dress him." His look made it clear that it might be a hopeless cause but they would do their best. "Then, we shall attend to your needs."

"Does that sound acceptable to both of you?" Jean asked.

"Sure," Pain answered. "I'll be the guinea pig. Let's see how well you can do."

Gino sniffed. "We can only do the best we can with what we have to work with."

"Then excuse me for a moment." Pain stood, left the room, opened one of the suitcases they had brought in, and returned a couple of minutes later holding his prize up.

"Whatever you choose has to go well with these."

The twins' faces fell.

"I am afraid you may have come to the wrong boutique, sir," Gino managed to squeak. "I am not sure that anything we have here goes well with those."

"Your assignment," he said firmly, "is to put together some outfits that do."

"You know…" Jean nodded and smiled at the new challenge. "I think we can."

Even Agony had been taken by surprise. Her partner held up a pair of polished black cowboy boots with silver stitching. They were very impressive but she had never seen them before and wondered why he thought this was the right time to put them to use.

Pain caught her look and with an apology in his eyes for not having clued his partner in earlier, he approached her and whispered, "According to Buchanan, I'm a rich asshole of a self-made real-estate mogul. What screams asshole louder than wearing cowboy boots to a black-tie affair?"

She took a moment to digest that information, then leaned back in her chair with a smile at her partner's reasoning.

"You heard the man," she informed the twins. "Make it work."

"Is there any chance you have bolos?" Pain added one more request. "I've never gotten the hang of bow-ties."

"Andrea isn't happy to admit it but yes, we do." Jean smiled. "We merely don't keep them out on display. Let's go, Gino." She slapped her twin's chest. "We have a cowboy to dress."

"You could have pulled the boots out earlier." Agony expressed both her annoyance and amusement once they were left alone.

"We're all going on improvisation here, right? I brought them along as a last-minute impulse."

"And not a bad one at that for an asshole mogul."

Now that they had a clear idea of what the big man wanted, the twins—with Agony helping to critique each outfit—had him all set and ready to go within the hour. That left almost two and a half hours to please the woman.

The associates returned to the sales floor and Pain resumed the earlier conversation.

"Buchanan is only giving us enough to get started with. He's playing this one close to the vest, handing out only one tidbit at a time. As the op unfolds, if he has a chance, he will probably try to feed us more."

"More as in a specific target?" Agony was beginning to regret her decision to be drawn in. "I'd like to know if he's on a fishing trip or a treasure hunt. If it's fishing, are we going after Moby Dick? And if it's a treasure hunt, should we keep our eyes out for a map that says *X marks the spot*?"

"I'd like to know that myself." He leaned back in his chair and closed his eyes, trying to mentally follow the clues. "He's running this ass-backward but I can understand why. He gives us a little rope but not enough for him to get hung with."

"And once we're balls-deep into this mess," she continued with the train of thought, "he'll feed us a little more rope, but only enough for us to use to help get ourselves out while we're too busy to be able to screw with him. He's playing a very dangerous game."

"And has played it well enough to have dragged us into it."

Pain voiced that last thought with no recrimination in his voice toward his partner who he had left the final decision to. She appreciated the effort.

"But he has, over the years," he continued his reasoning, "made more than one effort to bring down Ahjoomenoni, which we all know is a fool's errand. But someone with that kind of focused determination has earned the right to be taken seriously."

"Oh, my," Agony whispered as a new rack of outfits was wheeled in for her to try. "But it might be worth it all to wear those clothes for a few days."

As was the case with Pain, who tried an outfit on and stepped out for critiquing, she now did the same. She had saved him from making a couple of unfortunate mistakes, especially when it came to a snap-buttoned shirt with snap-button pockets and he was determined to do the same.

Toward the end, she came out of her dressing room wearing a midnight-blue slit skirt with a matching vest over a pale blue blouse.

The twins fawned over how good it looked on her.

"The belt's wrong." Her partner interrupted the adoration society.

"Wrong how?" Gino sniffed. "It is a light gray bordering on silver. Look how it can't help but draw attention to it."

"Exactly," agreed the cowboy. "Nothing should distract from the shades of blue. The belt needs to be black, bordering on an even darker shade of black. It should not outshine the rest of the ensemble."

Agony stepped back and took a second look in the mirror.

"You heard him, twinkle-twins. Bring me your best in black."

Richard and Sheri finished their shopping with enough time to pack their new clothes into the two suitcases, with the outfits they would wear that evening placed neatly on top while they waited for the limo. It was a two-hour drive to the Moorfin and they didn't want to get the outfits they would wear when they arrived all wrinkled. When they got close to the lodge, they would find a convenient place to change.

"Sorry if we were a little difficult to deal with," Agony told the twins as the limo driver loaded the two suitcases and the partners said farewell to the staff of Syeni.

"You two? Difficult?" Jean gave them both a smile.

"We can tell you about difficult." Gino also smiled.

"Have a safe trip and a good time," his sister called and waved at them as they stepped into the limo.

"Did everything go well?" Andrea came up behind them.

"Very well," Jean told the owner. The sister-twin had managed to enjoy herself.

"A charming couple," her brother lied.

Andrea watched as her two best sales associates helped themselves to a couple of single-serving bottles of Merlot from the refreshments table and headed to the back to enjoy their well-deserved lunch breaks.

CHAPTER ELEVEN

"Thoughts?" Agony asked as the chauffeur pulled out and started the two-hour drive to the lodge upstate.

"Great boutique. Wonderful staff. I feel ready to go. I only need to close my eyes and rest for a while. Driver?"

"Yes, sir?"

"Is the privacy window as dark as the outside windows? I need a short nap."

"This is your home for the next couple of hours," the man replied. "You two relax. Shopping can be such an exhausting experience, can it not?"

"Yes, it can." Pain appreciated the understanding. "We will want to make a quick stop when we get close to the lodge to allow us to change into our proper attire."

"Understood, sir." The driver sounded competent and confident. "I am very familiar with the area up there and know the perfect place. You two rest your minds now."

The window behind the driver slid up silently. Agony was about to say something but Pain put a finger to his lips to request silence for a moment as he searched through a pocket. He came up with a pen and a blank scheduling pad with the Syeni Boutique emblem engraved at the top of each page.

She watched as he scribbled.

Stole notepad. Limo rented by agent B. Don't trust listening devices not being in place.

She took the pad, read the note, and after a few minutes, scribbled her reply.

Your handwriting sucks. But instincts seem sound.

He read it and scribbled back.

TX.

They spent the next two hours thinking things through silently while occasionally scribbling and passing notes. Texting, Flintstones' style.

True to his word, as they neared the destination, the driver pulled into a good-sized multi-purpose service station. The station held pumps for gas, two different fast-food facilities, and a central store that could pass for a small supermarket and sold everything from munchies to motor oil.

The partners had several restrooms to choose from as they went their separate ways, freshened up as best they could, and changed into their casual late-afternoon attire.

They made a good-looking couple, the driver thought when his passengers returned and settled in for the last short leg of the drive.

He wanted to ask if they'd ever been to the Moorfin before, but the window between the cab and the backseats was still up and no one had requested that it be lowered.

From his experience, whether they were coming or going, no one whose destination was the Moorfin had ever seemed like the talkative type. It was their choice and allowed him to focus on his driving as he wound up through the hills. He was, after all, a very professional limo driver, and having his full attention on the road was his priority.

But he was also human and as such, was often curious about

his passengers. Many were the times he returned home after a shift to an evening meal or a late-night dinner or early breakfast, and his wife would ask him about his day or night and if anything interesting or entertaining had happened.

Many times, his stories were funny and she loved to hear him regale her with the details of what he had witnessed and overheard. But if he answered, "It was a Moorfin trip," his spouse of thirty-seven years would smile softly and say, "Booorrriiing."

"To the max," he would reply and they would fill the rest of their time talking about their three children and four grandkids' latest adventures and consider it quality time well spent.

The driver rolled the window down. "We are arriving now," he informed his passengers as he drove along the long tree-lined drive to the entrance of the Moorfin Lodge.

"Is this what they call a lodge in these parts?" Agony asked.

"Only in the humblest of terms," he informed her.

They had made good time and the sun was still four hours away from settling behind the western horizon. Wasn't daylight-savings time wonderful? The limo crested a slight hill and they were now on the downward sweep. The main lodge and its closest amenities were visible in a grand display of wealth and comfort.

"We may be underdressed," Agony muttered. She had never seen the likes of an estate like this before. Pain had, but it had been overseas and owned by an oil-baron sheik who had built a monument to himself in the middle of the sandy hills of a desert, with enough water pumped in to produce a lush, green landscape where none should be.

But that, he reminded himself, was a long-ago op and had nothing to do with this one.

"Can you pause here, please?" he asked. "I would like a moment to be able to take it all in."

"Understood," the driver answered. It wasn't the first time the question had been asked by people who had never been there before. A hundred feet ahead was a turn-off designed for such purposes. He pulled into it and parked.

"It is magnificent, isn't it?" he stated as he turned the engine off. "As a driver, I have been here hundreds of times—although never inside, of course—but I still remember the first time I crested the hill. This turn-off was designed precisely for first-time guests to enjoy a moment of quiet to take it all in. So please, feel free to step out and take all the time you need."

"Thank you." Pain stepped out on his side of the limo and Agony did the same from hers.

They approached the lodge-side edge of the turn-off, where there was an exquisite protective barrier made of stone, not concrete, to prevent anyone from stepping too far and tumbling down the hill. The hill was more sloping than steep, and the grass looked perfectly manicured. Anyone who took a step too far toward the edge would more likely end up with embarrassing grass stains as opposed to broken bones, but either one would cause a less than ideal appearance when they checked in. At the Moorfin, appearances were of the utmost importance—at least that was what Agent Buchanan had drilled into them.

"What separates this," she asked as she leaned on the stone wall and looked out and down at their next few days of existence, "from the country estate of an English prince?"

"The accents of the inhabitants?" Pain made his best guess.

The whole estate was situated around a lake that nestled among gently rolling hills and woodlands as far as the eye could see. Surprisingly, the lakeside hadn't been developed except for six buildings that looked small from a distance, but each one had a dock that led directly to the water. Several of the docks had boats tied up alongside them. The craft did not seem designed for fishing.

Three wings comprised the lodge itself and each of them was built along the edge of a pool that looked large enough to have its own zip code. Each room facing it included a balcony that could hold a cook-out for twelve.

"What are those small blue things next to the big pool?" Agony muttered with a frown.

"A kiddie pool, a beginner pool, and a couple of bunny pools," Pain guessed.

"What the hell is a bunny pool?"

"You've never done much skiing, have you?"

"I wanted to once," she told him. "But when I was a kid, I heard that Cher's first husband got into an argument with a tree while skiing. The tree won, so I marked that off my list of things to do."

"The point is to learn how to swim before diving into the deep end of a pool."

"There you go again, trying to sound all kinds of profound."

"That's right." Pain smiled as he answered and kept his focus on their destination. "The Dalai Lama lives in fear of me overtaking him. We call each other every week to see which of us has come up with the best one-line advice."

"Next time you talk to him, tell him I said hi and will catch up with him in my next life."

Agony had seen and heard enough. He followed in her wake as she strode to the limo. There was only one way to proceed and that was to get inside the grand estate.

"We're ready," he informed the driver.

"If you say so, sir." The man had his doubts.

The driver delivered them to the front entrance of the lodge, where three attendants fought over the two suitcases. One couple with only two suitcases? How were they supposed to earn any tips when they didn't each have at least two bags to carry?

Someone clapped loudly and ended the attendants' squabble.

"Cottage four," the concierge instructed firmly.

"Yes, sir," one of them answered as he and the other winning luggage carrier made off with their prizes. The third tried to accept his defeat gracefully and walked quietly to his station.

"Thank you, Matthew." The man spoke first to the driver. "I hope your return drive home is safe and uneventful."

He didn't wait for a response as he turned his full attention to the new arrivals.

"I am Earnest," he informed them, "in both name and temperament. You must be Richard and Sheri, and I have the pleasure of welcoming you to the Moorfin."

"Thanks, Ernie." Pain dove into his role as a major-league jerk and slapped the man on his shoulder as if they had been best friends forever. "Which way to the booze?"

He didn't wait for an answer and headed inside.

"I am supposed to show you to your cottage first," the concierge pleaded with Agony.

"And you will," she assured him with a sigh for the ages, "as soon as my husband makes his grand entrance."

Earnest followed Sheri, who stalked after her husband into the lobby of the Moorfin, where a pre-dinner cocktail hour seemed to be in full swing.

She caught up with Pain before he had a chance to open his mouth to boldly announce himself to the assembly and jammed a fingernail into the back of his neck. The way all good spouses do, she took hold of his elbow and spoke sharply into his ear.

"I know it's hard for you, but don't overdo the asshole routine too soon."

"Too much?" he asked.

"Not yet," she replied, "but don't push it."

The happy couple stood still, arm in arm, and faced the early-hour cocktail crowd. They caught several glances cast at them. None of them showed any concern but several looked, for lack of a better word, hungry.

"Please." Earnest hurried to them. "It is a long drive to get here, so let me show you to your cottage first before you begin socializing."

"Our cottage?" Pain tried to keep the surprise out of his voice. Buchanan hadn't said anything about a cottage.

"One of our finest. Your carriage is waiting."

"Our carriage?" Agony responded.

"It is more like a glorified golf cart," the concierge replied with a wink and a smile. "But after your long trip here, it is the easiest way to help guide the cottage guests to their temporary home away from home so they can settle in."

"I'm sorry, hoss." Pain shuffled his silver-stitched black cowboy boots in a friendly manner and stopped short of trying to pull off a Texas accent. "But we have plenty of time to settle in. I am a developer of high-end buildings and the lodge appears to be a fine work of art. Can you give us a quick tour of it first?"

"But of course, Richard," he agreed.

"Please, call me Dick." He echoed Earnest's opening line when he had greeted them. "A Dick by name and a dick by nature, ain't that right, hon?"

"Trust him, Earnest," she responded acidly, "he has that one right."

"Alrighty then." The concierge knew how to appease every request. "A walking tour of the lodge it is, and I can assure you that the walking part of the tour won't take too long. Then, we shall retrieve your carriage. There is considerable ground to cover at the Moorfin."

The walking tour never left the first floor.

"Every room above the first floor is private," their guide explained as he led them down a hallway and opened a couple of doors along the way. "The first floor is dedicated to group activities, some of which you may wish to join and some of which you may not. The activities are designed to appeal to specific tastes, and wouldn't it be a boring world if everyone's taste was the same?"

"That does sound like a very gray kind of world," Agony agreed.

"Exactly." The man nodded. "The events are scheduled in advance and participation is entirely up to each guest's discretion. The Moorfin prides itself on being a no-judgment zone."

"A judgment-free zone." The unscrupulous real-estate developer in cowboy boots sounded happy. "I like that."

"You would." Agony had slid into her Sheri persona.

"And you wouldn't?" Dick sniped in return.

"Earnest?" Sheri damn near commanded. "Some fresh air, please."

The earnest concierge led them to the closest door that opened onto the very expansive pool area.

"Now that there," Dick stated, "is a lot of water."

The partners stared at the main pool and the various smaller ones they had observed from the turn-off this side of the crest in the hill where their limo driver had pulled into. Now that they had a closer view, they learned that there were no kiddie pools and everything seemed to be clothing optional.

"I think I'm ready for that buggy ride to our cottage now."

"He means our carriage ride." She corrected her pompous husband and decided that Sheri was an easy role to master as long as Pain played her easy-to-hate husband. No method acting was needed.

Earnest walked them through the lodge and guided them into the back seats of the glorified golf cart. He continued the tour as best he could as he drove toward the cottage where he would be oh, so happy to drop them off. He was the head concierge of the Moorfin and knew his duties, which were to cater to every whim —within reason—of the guests, no matter how pompous and arrogant they were.

"If you look there," he pointed out as he drove, "you can see a few smaller outbuildings around the lake and several trails that lead off from them."

"The buildings," Dick, the dick real-estate developer seized the moment, "must have a very vital purpose. Otherwise, the space might be better used for vacation condo development. That is some prime property right there."

"Yes," Earnest agreed and continued to explain as if he was nothing more than a simple tour guide. "Among the buildings, there is a stable for some of the finest horses that never had to spend a day of their lives competing against each other on man-made racetracks. There is also a kennel that houses every kind of hunting dog ever bred."

"And you keep the horses and dogs locked up all day?" Agony couldn't prevent herself from asking before Dick the dick kicked her ankle in an effort to remind her that she was supposed to be a bitch.

"Oh no." Earnest laughed. "There is a hunt here almost every day. The Moorfin lodge is located in the center of several hundred square miles of private property. There are no hunting season restrictions here. If it moves, it can be killed. Another building houses all the ATVs in case someone prefers a more modern mode of transportation while out on a hunt. But that reminds me. Have you had a chance to read through your welcome packet yet?"

"Well, no." Dick was short with his answer. "How could we, when we haven't been given one yet?"

"Someone must have dropped the ball on that one." The man looked apologetic. "I'll have one delivered to your cottage. The only thing of concern since we are talking about hunting and things like that is that all guests must present any firearms they bring onto the property to the hunt master upon arrival. That allows him to keep them safe in his armory and dispense them accordingly."

"Weapons? A hunt master?" Sheri the ruthless heiress

snapped. "Do I look like someone who is carrying anything resembling a hidden weapon?"

"Trust me, Ernie," her husband interjected. "The only hidden weapon she has is her tongue. It can cut like a razor blade up close or throw fire from a distance. It might be lethal but it's not the kind of weapon that can be locked up in some hunt master's box, although I do truly sometimes wish it could."

The partners gave each other a quick wink, satisfied that they had prevented Earnest from learning that Agony had her S&W and a backup strapped to her ankles, not to mention her baton. Pain had lost track of the places his partner had been able to hide her baton.

"And besides," he added, "When it comes down to handling wild beasts, I prefer a hands-on approach."

"He does have many faults," Sheri was happy to acknowledge, "but the use of his hands is not one of them."

The conversation had lasted long enough for Earnest to drive the carriage to the front of cottage number four, where he stopped to let them out.

"I suspect"—his eyebrows did a pathetic excuse of a waggle—"that you two will feel right at home here."

"Thanks, Ernie." Dick climbed out of the carriage and walked to the door.

"Has anyone ever told you," Sheri said to the concierge as she stepped out, "that you would look good with a pencil-thin mustache?"

Having never been able to grow a mustache, he missed the reference to how tacky a pencil-thin one would look on the wrong face and drove the carriage away. He was convinced that he had received a compliment from an extremely hot chick who was married to someone who was completely wrong for her. From there, it was easy to remind himself that one day, if he played everything right, he would most certainly score.

After watching the rather odious concierge drive the carriage toward the big house, the partners studied the cottage from the outside.

"How much discretionary funds does Buchanan get on a yearly basis?" Pain wondered.

"Our tax dollars at work." Agony sighed as they walked inside.

Their suitcases had been delivered and placed to the side of the entryway.

"When I was a kid," Pain said as he scanned the luxurious interior, "a cottage was a small rustic affair that you would rent for a week as a vacation getaway. There would be one bedroom for the parents, maybe a second small bedroom to pile all the kids into, and a sleeper-sofa to handle any overflow. And no matter the season, it would always smell a little musty."

"Listen to you whine," Agony chided. "My dad didn't believe in staying in a place where other people had been. Our vacations were spent in tents at campgrounds. Nice tents, granted, but still tents."

The living room was spacious enough to host a party for twelve with seating left over and featured a stone fireplace and in-wall entertainment center. They left their suitcases where they were and Pain began a self-guided tour while Agony took a minute to get out of her snooty heiress persona pout and strut.

How do the Instagram rich-bitches do it? she wondered. *Do they have to practice how to act like a snoot-chute, or does it come naturally to them?*

She was about to ask her partner when he emerged from the bedroom holding several listening and recording devices he had found when, out of habit, he'd swept the room.

"Really...umm...Dick?"

"Indeed...Princess."

"Can you do the bathroom next?" She switched back to pouty heiress mode in order to keep up appearances for anyone who was watching and listening. "I need to tinkle and tinkle right now!"

Five minutes later, he came out of the bathroom holding a smaller handful of electronics.

"That information was not included in the brochure my assistant gave me." She didn't have to act at sounding pissed. "As soon as we get back, I will send her to the unemployment line!"

Agony stormed angrily toward the bathroom. She did have to pee and the sooner the better.

Pain swept the rest of the rooms and had shoved everything into a garbage bag by the time his partner returned.

"Do you think you got them all?" she asked.

"Life has no guarantees, my darling," the heiress's husband responded through gritted teeth in case he'd missed a bug.

She heaved a mighty sigh. "It would be just like you to miss something."

Their stay at the Moorfin was off to a great start.

CHAPTER TWELVE

The odious concierge having taken the carriage to the main lodge, Agony followed Pain and the plastic garbage bag full of electronics out of the cottage and down to the dock. Walking to the far end of it, he flung the offending equipment as far out into the lake as he could. They watched as the bag landed in the water, bobbed for a couple of minutes, and sank.

"You always have to remember to poke holes in the plastic," he explained. "Otherwise, the damn bags will simply float and float and float."

"I'll have to remember that. Body-part disposal 101. Do you think you got all the bugs out of the cottage?"

"Hell if I know for sure," he admitted. "I think I did but I wouldn't bet against even the bugs out here being bugged."

"Now that's a reassuring thought."

They turned toward home not quite sweet temporary home.

"I think I found them all." Pain sighed and hoped he was right. "Because if I didn't, we may as well put an end to the op right now. We need to be able to talk and not as Dick the dick and Sheri."

"We'll have to trust that you did." Agony didn't doubt that he had. She hadn't even thought to sweep for bugs.

Back in their cottage, hoping that all the surveillance devices were removed, they decided now was the time to find out if they could talk freely. If they couldn't, the entire op would come crashing to a sudden stop and it would be best to know that as soon as possible.

"I have never felt so icky in my life." She was the first to speak. "I'll take the main bedroom and a quick rinse-off shower. See you in ten."

She lugged her suitcase into her room and true to her word, was back in ten minutes, wearing another casual outfit that both the twins at the Syeni Boutique had raved over. The ten minutes gave him the time to haul his suitcase to his room and return and start scanning.

"That was quick," he observed as she joined him.

"Why waste water when all I needed was a quick rinse? Did you find anything interesting?"

"You tell me." He handed her a laminated tri-fold brochure of activities that had been compiled to help them decide which organized activities they would be interested in.

"Huh." She studied it with a small frown. "Nothing is listed here for when the sun is rising or high in the sky."

"You noticed that too?"

"Munchies at midnight." She read parts of the menu aloud. "After dinner delights. Sundown-pants down—and what the fuck is a Tantric Banquet?"

"If you have to ask, you don't want to know," Pain replied.

"I know what fucking tantric means." She scowled and shook her head. "It's the banquet part I'm confused about. Does it mean that instead of chicken wings, it'll be a table spread with deep-fried thumbs and assorted dipping sauces?"

"Your guess is as good as mine," was the only answer Pain could come up with. "I'll take a quick rinse-off shower and then maybe we should head to the pool. The temperature is still in the eighties and the sun is an hour away from setting. From what we saw from the ridge, the pool is where the Moorfin's guests like to congregate between events."

"I agree." She acknowledged her partner's logic. "You take your rinse-off. I have a call to make to our sponsor."

"Good luck with that."

He wandered to his room and rinse-off and she pulled out a very old flip phone that Buchanan had given them to use. The technology was so out of date that he was able to use it to easily route secure calls through a satellite that the feds had paid a small fortune to keep it circling the globe and be held in reserve for very special occasions.

Their tax dollars at work again.

"Have you found anything yet?" He answered on the second ring.

"Only a lot of creepy," Agony answered. This was not the time for chit-chat.

"I wish I could say I was surprised."

"You have set us up three ways to Sunday." She made it clear that she was not pleased.

"Yes, I did," Buchanan replied without one note of apology in his voice. "But I wouldn't have if I didn't think you two could handle it."

Agony was about to tell Special Agent Marshal Buchanan the specific details of how she would break every bone in his body and in which order she would break them when a loud knocking came from the cottage's door.

"Shit!" she exclaimed and in her next breath, informed the agent, "Don't expect another call anytime soon!"

She flipped the phone shut and stashed it under a cushion before she strode to the door.

"What?" she demanded, thinking it would be Earnest Ernie

making a return trip to inform them of another minor Moorfin regulation he had forgotten to mention.

"Hardy har har and well met!"

Standing in front of her was a man short of sixty but well past his fiftieth birthday. He wore Bermuda shorts and an almost matching shirt that was completely unbuttoned but hey, what was a little belly fat amongst friends?

Aviator sunglasses were perched on his head. In one hand, he held a tumbler of what smelled like rum. In the other, he held a large, wet garbage bag with a few drops of water still leaking out of it. He set the bag outside but kept the tumbler in his hand and strode inside without waiting for an invitation.

"I'm Chauncey." He introduced himself blithely. "My friends call me Chance. And you, my dear, are?"

"Agon—" She caught herself in time and faked a cough. "Sheri. Sorry, I had something caught in my throat."

"Don't we all get something caught in our throats at one time or another?" He chuckled. "Especially here at the Moorfin." That comment drew another chuckle.

His appearance and chuckling aside, the one thing that shocked her the most was that the man who had entered the cottage was Chauncey Morris, the dignified chief of police in the city who was the superior officer everyone answered to. She had only met him once and that had been when he pinned the detective badge on her uniform as she was being promoted. He had also been in the background at a couple of meetings that led to her dismissal from the force, but this didn't seem like the right time to remind him of that and she hoped he didn't recognize her.

"Sheri and share alike." The police chief giggled at his play on words and she realized she had no worries in the personal recognition department. His gaze was too busy focusing on every part of her body other than her face.

"What can I do for you, Chance?" She looked confused.

"Well..." He took another sip from his tumbler. "The first thing you and Rick-a-dicka-doodle can do is to stop tossing very expensive electronic equipment into the lake."

He pointed outside to the water-soaked garbage bag that was almost at the end of its leakage issue.

"Oh, yeah. Dick can be such a dick sometimes," she muttered. "I tried to tell him—"

"Tried to tell him what?" Dick hurried into the room wearing only a pair of shorts. He had heard the voices and hurried out as quickly as he could, a towel draped over his shirtless shoulders. "And what the hell is going on out here?"

"I tried to tell you," his bitch of a wife informed him, "that you are sometimes too paranoid for your own good. This is the city's chief of police, Chauncey...umm?"

"Chauncey Morris." The chief extended the hand that wasn't holding the tumbler. "But at the Moorfin, I am simply called Chance."

"Pleased to meet you, Chance." Pain had no choice but to shake his hand. "What brings you to our humble abode?"

"Earnest Ernie." the buttoned-down police chief Agony was familiar with, who was barely buttoned at all at the moment, started to explain jovially. "He suggested that I welcome you personally and also"—he pointed to the soggy bag of electronics outside the door—"maybe help clarify a few things, especially since this is your first visit here and maybe you missed something in the brochure when you booked your stay."

The chief took an uninvited step farther into the room and turned in a slow circle. "Cottage number four. One of the best. Ohh." He giggled. "If these walls could talk."

"It seems to me," Dick said through gritted teeth, "that the walls can see and hear, so it wouldn't surprise me if they could also talk."

"But that's the point." Chance's voice held no hint of reprimand over what must have been a simple misunderstanding that led to the destruction of the electronics. "The entire lodge is discreetly wired for both sound and video. It is one of its most attractive features and is greatly appreciated by the guests who, after their stay has ended, enjoy reliving all the lodge's activities while they were here. There's nothing like a little keepsake to be able to remember what a good time was had by all."

"So..." Agony wanted to believe that she hadn't heard the head-honcho of the city's entire police force right. "Everything that the dick and I do will be recorded for any and everyone to be able to view after they get home?"

"Everything." He scrutinized the good-looking albeit bickering couple and smiled. "And now that I see what the goods are, I can assure you that the two of you will make several top-ten lists."

He handed Sheri his tumbler and continued.

"If we all hang together and if you'll excuse my patriotic warbling..." The chief chuckled again as if he had said something funny. "Then there is no need for any worries. I understand that you may feel a little shy your first time here but hell, I'm a well-respected chief of police so I have more to lose than almost anyone else here, but look at me!"

Without any further warning, dignified Chauncey Morris dropped his shorts and shucked his shirt. He held his arms out and made a three-sixty turn so neither of the new arrivals would miss anything.

"See? Free as a bird. Oh, and notice, no tan lines anywhere."

The partners had no desire to notice anything but it was hard not to when a naked man twirled so close in front of them. He put his hands behind his head and performed an odd gyration that he must have thought was seductively sexy, not that he had much in the gyrating department.

His welcome and performance over, Chance scooped his clothes from the floor and took his tumbler from Sheri.

"Now that we're all friends, how's about you two finish freshening up and join us poolside when you're ready? I think you'll like it here, and I am very sure that everyone here will like you."

He gave them both suggestive winks and ambled out and toward the main lodge, still buck-ass naked.

"Oh," he called over his shoulder, "don't worry about the electronics. We'll chalk it up to an accident and have them all replaced in a jiffy. No one will want to miss anything you two might get up to."

Agony closed the door and leaned back against it.

"I think I need another shower now."

"Is there any chance you have something that can wash my eyes out?" Pain asked. "I think they might be bleeding."

"We may as well face the music sooner rather than later," Pain said and resigned himself to forgoing an eye-wash. "Let me find a shirt and we'll go to the pool while there's still some sun. What the fuck has Buchanan gotten us into?"

Ten minutes later, they were walking toward the pool area.

"I'm telling you, Pain." Agony felt free to talk as they walked. "That's not the Chauncey Morris I observed while on the force. He was the most straight-laced stick-up-his-ass commander you could imagine. Something has gotten into him."

"That's an interesting phrase." He referred to her last words. "Something has gotten into him. I would guess a large variety of pharmaceuticals."

She didn't have time to pursue that line of reasoning because the occupants of cottage three joined them on the path to the pool. They were a younger couple and were so obviously besotted with each other and a little unsteady on their feet that they didn't even bother to introduce themselves. When they reached the pool a couple of minutes later, their walking companions made an immediate bee-line for the water and shed all their clothes before they jumped in and joined the party.

The larger part of the pool consisted of a shallow end where the swimmers could stand on their feet while bouncing around if that was their preference. Dozens of floatation devices with cupholders were still being deployed, the better to be able to splash and drink at the same time.

"Don't you dare leave my side," Agony ordered.

"Why would I want to do that? I'm scared shitless here and am counting on you for protection."

"Dick the dick and Sheri share alike!" Chance bellowed a greeting.

The police chief climbed out of his section of the pool party and joined them to begin introductions to some of the others gathered on the expansive poolside deck. She didn't know if the water in the pool was warm or cold but it certainly didn't do the chief's Big Chief any favors.

She noted that a large number of the poolside guests he introduced them to were middle-aged women fighting off middle-aged appearances with a vengeance, which explained why they hadn't ventured into the pool. Water and cosmetics were never a good combination.

Her surreptitious scrutiny revealed the fact that her partner seemed to be a sight for several sore, overly made up eyes. Seeing Pain standing next to Chauncey Morris, she could understand the preference and made a vow to do her best to honor his request to be able to count on her as his protector.

These contemplations were interrupted by the tinkling of several small bells that announced a new addition to the scene. One could be forgiven if they had a flashback to childhood when on hot summer days, the ice cream truck rolled down the street, music blaring, and all the kids flocked to it. The tinkling of the bells let everyone know that it was time to come and get some dessert.

The trolley had arrived.

It was a handcart only in the sense that it was pushed by hand. The young, bikini-clad woman who operated it was certainly not peddling flowers, nor was her Speedo-clad assistant. It was four feet in height and the top was loaded with a vast assortment of beverages, most of them alcoholic.

Speedo-boy's job was to pour the beverages into whatever plastic glasses were handed to him since actual glass wasn't allowed on the concrete deck. Up the left side of the trolley were shelves filled with one-serving bags of what could only be pharmaceutical munchies, a snack rack free for the taking.

The right side of the trolley also provided shelves full of munchies, equally free for the taking.

To Agony, it looked like a truck full of Skittle's had dumped its load into it. Red, yellow, green, blue, orange, and purple? She noticed that Chance scooped up a fair number of the pale blue ones, popped them into his mouth like candy, and washed them down with a drink of whatever Speedo-boy had handed him.

Don't be blue, just take a blue. She remembered the late-night commercials that always ended with a quick warning to consult your doctor before taking to make sure your heart was strong enough to handle the activity.

"So, tall, dark, and handsome." One of the ladies took hold of Pain's arm and tried to separate him from the herd. "Which of tonight's activities takes your fancy?"

"No fair." Another one took hold of Pain's other arm. "I called dibs."

"I called it first!" a third woman interjected.

"No!" Sheri and share alike informed them. "I called dibs first on this one. Didn't I, Dick?"

"I'm afraid she's right, ladies." He tried to look apologetic. "First come, first served."

He knew he would have to pay for it later, but he patted Agony's behind as he looked back with a wink and a smile while he allowed her to drag him away from the gaggle of carnivorous creatures.

"Sorry about the ass-tap," he apologized before she unleashed her indignation.

She opened her mouth to respond but a voice rang out to distract them.

"Look what I found!" the naked Chance announced to one and all. The blue pills appeared to be more fast-acting than the over-the-counter kind. "Who's up for a little full-contact swim?"

It seemed the chief hadn't been the only one who had snatched a handful of blues from the trolley. Several other men tossed their towels aside, displayed their wares, and grasped every female's hand they could find before they jumped in the pool to join the festivities.

"Aw, what the hell," one of the still dry, well-made up women announced to the gaggle. "We'd better get it while the getting's good."

Clothes were flung on the poolside and naked bodies splashed into the water.

"Creepy guy watching." Agony let the ass-tap slide. This wasn't her first undercover dance.

"You'll have to be a little more specific." Pain leaned down as if whispering sweet nothings in her ear. "We are surrounded by creepy guys."

"Back porch of the lodge," she murmured into her partner's ear, certain that the pool area would have numerous hidden mics. "Bald head, gray beard, and a cigar. He's keeping an eye on everything."

"Are you ready to get naked?" he asked as he noticed a twelve-person bubbling hot tub with only six occupants.

"Are you ready to die?"

"Always." Pain chuckled. "But preferably not today. Unfortunately, we can't simply stand here. It's time to get wet."

He scooped her into his arms and strode to the hot tub and she kicked and screamed all the way.

"Have I ever told you that you're a great actress?"

"I am not acting!" she snapped.

"Sure you are, Sheri."

He reached the tub, Sheri still bitching up a storm, and Dick the dick announced to the occupants, "We are virgins here so we're taking it one step at a time. Got room in there for two more?"

"It's a virgin toss!" a man called from the tub.

"Virgin toss! Virgin toss!" The chorus rose from the three naked couples.

"A double-dip on the virgin part," Dick responded as he leapt into the bubbling water with Agony still in his arms.

They both came up spluttering but at least remained clothed as they scrambled to find seats next to each other.

"We can't stay but for only a tick," he said.

"Then you gotta try a few of the yellows the next time the trolley rolls through," another man replied, followed by a couple of female giggles.

The partners stayed long enough to hope that they had lost the focus of the graybeard with the cigar, thankful that the water bubbled enough to obscure their view of what was going on down below. The time in the tub also enabled a few short conversations with the other tubbers, mostly about who was who and who did what as far as day jobs went. They weren't in-depth discussions, but everyone was jovial and they at least gave the partners a little more info, including some juicy gossip regarding the Moorfin.

"Didn't I tell you, babe, that this place would be great!" Pain said as he dove and came up with Agony slung over a shoulder, found the steps leading out of the tub, and marched through the pool area.

Every other word out of Sheri's mouth was "Fuck!" as Dick

kept her slung over his shoulder and navigated between the other guests, past the prying eyes of the cigar-smoking-graybeard, and toward their cottage.

"Now that," someone from the pool deck said, "is what I call a happy couple."

"Ahhh, to be young and so in love," another agreed.

"Why don't you do that to me anymore, Henry?"

"Don't blame me," Henry was quick to reply. "Blame it on my sciatica."

"I think it's safe to put me down now," Agony informed him not so gently after they were out of range of spying eyes.

"Yeah, right." Pain slung her off his shoulders and onto her feet. "Sorry about that."

"No problem," she lied as they continued toward their cottage and hoped that the electronics hadn't been installed yet.

"You could have slung me over your shoulder anytime you wanted." He defended his actions.

"And I might have if I didn't have to fight off half a dozen matrons for the honor."

"They are a feisty bunch, aren't they?" He attempted a touch of humor that did not have the desired effect on his partner. "But hey, did I get you in and out of the hot tub with all your clothing still intact?"

Agony admitted grudgingly that he had, but that didn't mean she wasn't still pissed. They reached the cottage, her footsteps having hit the ground a little harder than her partner's along the way. The wet bag of electronics was still outside the door.

"Do you need to sweep again?" she asked, still feeling the sense that her privacy had been invaded earlier by the electronics' intrusion and wanting to be able to talk freely once they got inside.

"Sweep for what?" Pain laughed. "You heard Chance. We're all friends here."

He urged her inside and pressed a finger to her lips to keep her quiet while he made another scan of the cottage, both inside and out, before he returned.

"We're all good," he announced. "At least for now. My best guess is that it will take the Moorfin at least two days to replace the electronics. "Let's decide how we want to spend the rest of our day."

"As far as I can make out from the menu," she answered, "a day at the Moorfin doesn't begin until the sun goes down."

Pain nodded. "Without us having the benefits of the pharmaceuticals, they will be a hard group to keep up with if we have to party the night away with them."

"I need another quick rinse-off shower before I feel decent again." She sounded firm. "I don't care how hot the water was in that tub, I'm not convinced that I am icky-free."

"I hear you," he agreed. "I'll meet you here in an hour, dressed in our evening's finest?"

"Make it an hour and a half. I'll wear my dark-blue ensemble. Try not to match. We do, after all, have to keep up appearances...Dick."

CHAPTER THIRTEEN

At ten o'clock, Pain reappeared in the main room wearing a slightly puffy white shirt and purple jeans. These were accessorized by a wide silver belt with an outlandish turquoise buckle that matched his bolo-string tie. The jeans weren't boot-cut and the bottom of each leg was tucked inside his black with silver stitching cowboy boots.

Agony, as promised, emerged wearing her midnight-blue slit skirt and vest over the pale blue blouse, along with the solid black belt he had insisted on when the outfit was being put together. She found him looking over the menu of the night's activities and shaking his head.

"I do need to get something to eat but I will not go anywhere near the Tantric Banquet," he declared firmly.

She focused on the menu and pointed at an entry. "The lodge has a Grab & Go Café."

"Grab what and go where?"

"There's only one way to find out."

Pain wasn't thrilled with the suggestion but it seemed like the best option. "The main event seems to be the Bacchanalian Ballet.

It starts at midnight, so maybe we can hope to find some actual food at the café and then make an appearance at the ballet?"

She reached under the cushion where she'd stashed the flip phone quickly when the chief had arrived and pulled it out. "It sounds like as good a plan as any but right now, I have an agent to call."

"Special Agent," he reminded her.

"Special my ass." She pressed redial and found the speaker button.

"Talk to me." Buchanan answered on the second ring again.

"And say what? Thanks for sending us to the droopy, dangling, sicko-fuckhut? Were you aware that every room here is wired for sound and video?"

"No. Having never been there, I wasn't aware of that. But it could come in useful if I ever get the authority to set up a raid."

"A raid for what? As far as I know, having a limp-dick is not a criminal offense, and the various pills used to activate said dicks would be a misdemeanor at best."

He didn't sound at all offended by her rebukes and asked calmly, "Can we set your ranting aside for a moment? That way, maybe you can tell me if you have made any connections yet."

"The only connection I want to make right now is my boot with your head!"

"Is Pain there?" Buchanan hoped for a calmer report.

"Yeah. I'm right here and rooting for her boot to make solid contact."

"I sense that I don't have any friends in the room at the moment."

Agony snorted. "Look up the definition of friends in a dictionary and then tell me the last time you had anyone like that."

Pain took over as his partner stormed to a corner looking for all the world as if she wished she was in an octagon with Buchanan. "So far, the only people we've met are the city's police chief and Agony's former head-honcho, Chauncey call me

Chance Morris, and half a dozen wealthy bankers, investors, and some CEO types."

"Don't forget the wives, mistresses, and other hungry on the prowl vixens." She wanted to make it clear that there were also some women there who might have an agenda of their own.

He continued his report. "Everyone gives off the appearance of being wealthy and yes, no doubt most of them are, but powerful? They didn't strike me as that. These folks seem much more interested in popping pills and partying in the friendly confines of the Moorfin than they are in doing anything sinister."

Buchanan held fast to his convictions. "Well, someone there is. Forget about the small-timers. You two are professionals. Surely something or someone must have stood out."

Agony shrugged dismissively. "The only one who stood out to me was a creepy graybeard cigar smoker who watched everything from the confines of the deck of his room at the lodge."

"Why did he stand out?" The agent suddenly sounded interested.

She tried to explain the creepies Graybeard gave her. "Because while everyone else was partying, he sat on his own and watched from a distance. This place is a peeping-tom paradise. You don't even need to sneak up to any windows because everything here seems to be done for public consumption and entertainment."

"There you go, then." He sounded as if they'd at least found one target to focus on. "Does Graybeard have a name?"

"We didn't get close enough to ask and I'm not sure I want to."

"Which is why you need to. When is the next opportunity?"

Pain explained their itinerary. "After a quick hunt for food, we were hoping to keep our vomiting in check and head to the Bacchanalian Ballet at midnight. Not that we're looking forward to it. I'm telling you, Buchanan, this place is packed with nothing but creepy crawlies, and I'm not sure they are worth your attention."

"And why is that?" Special Agent Buchanan let his lack of addressing him properly slide.

"They all seem like overpriced lightweights."

"It sounds like a perfect place for a heavyweight to hide."

"Hiding in plain sight." He grudgingly acknowledged the agent's point.

Buchanan was pleased that he agreed with him for once. "Exactly. Go ahead and hit whatever the hell the ballet is and keep an eye out for Graybeard. My guess is that he is not too far from the bloodline of Blackbeard the Pirate, so watch your backs."

Agony joined the conversation again with a voice dripping acid. "Oh, golly, we are both so touched by your concern."

She flipped the phone shut, determined to have the last word as she ended the call.

"What?" she asked as she looked for another hiding place to stash the device.

Pain smiled. "There is nothing more satisfying than hanging up on an asshole who is under the misassumption that he is a superior."

"Oh, he is a superior all right. A superior…a superior…" She searched for a word that would describe the agent without using any of the words she had already used. "A superior pile of steaming puppy poop."

He laughed. "I like that. Special Agent Puppy Poop Buchanan."

"It does have a certain ring to it, doesn't it?" She laughed for the first time since they had taken the Moorfin assignment.

They brought their laugher under control and he asked. "Café first and then the ballet?"

"Have you ever been to a ballet before?" She was curious.

"I can't say I have. You?"

"Not since I was six. It was Swan Lake."

"Your parents took you to see Swan Lake when you were six?" Pain was impressed with his partner's parents.

"They didn't have much of a choice. It was at a children's ballet recital and I was playing the swan, complete with white tights, a tutu, and pointe shoes."

"I'm sorry I missed it. How did it go?"

"It went fine until the eight-year-old who was supposed to lift me in the third movement grabbed more ass than legs. I gave his face a kick that landed him in his orthodontist's office and my parents decided that ballet might not be a good career choice. Next stop, soccer camp. Any more questions?"

"None from me, except for how did it feel for a six-year-old girl to kick an eight-year-old boy's teeth in?"

The smile she gave made the words unnecessary, but she spoke them anyway. "Extremely satisfying. Café followed by the ballet?"

"I believe those are our instructions, Sheri."

"Then lead on, Dick."

Back in undercover mode, the Moorfin virgins found the Grab & Go Café, which fortunately did serve food. One roast beef on toasted rye and a grilled chicken sandwich later, they located the large hall where the ballet was about to start.

They were in the room for all of ten seconds before Pain offered his pre-ballet review. "I get the feeling that this won't be a Swan Lake our parents would recognize."

In the center of the large hall was a circular stage that rose only a foot above the floor. Curtains covered it, while the lighting in the room gave off a soft golden glow and revealed the ballet connoisseurs circling and mingling, all with drinks in hand.

The music started and the lights dimmed, but only slightly, as the curtains rose. The stage was lit by bright blue lights, the better to see the performers in. The lighting gave all the dancers' skins a pale appearance, but their clothing had been chosen to contrast with it so every article was visible. Not that there was much of it. The dancers' genitalia were barely covered, and the females had only a strip of cloth that wrapped tightly around their breasts.

They were graceful and athletic but it didn't take long for Dick and Sheri to realize that the movements weren't designed to appeal to the viewers' sense of the aesthetic as much as it leaned toward crude sexuality with a touch of Greco-Roman flavoring.

More than a little wary, the partners stuck together and wound through the crowd that had surrounded the stage, many of them looking as if they were about to drop their cumbersome clothing and join the dancers. Thankfully for all concerned, the crowd obeyed the look but don't touch rule.

Agony whispered into her partner's ear, "At least with the ballet, I don't have to watch the wobbly ones at the pool slapping their whatevers together."

"Thank God for small favors," Pain replied as he skirted a couple of enthusiastic women. He managed to not overreact and kept moving as he informed her that he'd had his first ass-grab of the evening.

"Let me know if you need my baton to help you fight them off," she told him.

"It does seem like a rather boisterous crowd." He declined the baton offer although it was extremely tempting. He wasn't experienced at attending ballets, but he didn't think that whistles and cat-calls from the audience were the standard response from the genteel set of people who usually attended them.

"As long as the audience keeps most of their clothes on and their hands off my ass, I think I can deal with it," she asserted. "At least long enough to reach the cottage before my stomach revolts and throws up my sandwich."

"Graybeard, two-o'clock." Pain nodded toward a far corner of the room where he saw the man with his ever-present cigar talking to police chief Chance and two other men. All four of them looked properly dressed for a civilized evening out.

Agony glanced at the group. "They don't seem particularly happy."

"Nope, they don't. But it doesn't seem to have anything to do with the performances on stage."

She allowed herself another glance at the foursome but it was one too many. Graybeard caught her eye and gave her a nod, a brief smile, and the touch of a wink. She didn't get the sense that it was a flirting moment so much as one predator acknowledging another.

It unsettled her but she didn't react to the smile or the wink. Instead, she instructed Pain to grasp her left thigh and left shoulder, hold her above his head, and turn in slow circles as if they were mimicking one of the ballet partners' moves.

He did as instructed and hoisted her above his head a second later. She was horizontally prone and firm as he started to rotate.

"And we're doing this why?" he asked conversationally.

"He caught me glancing at him. Oh, and smile. We are supposed to be having fun."

"I'm having the time of my life. I'm merely not sure why." He continued his slow rotation.

"I can't stare since he is aware of me. But something's going on over there. As long as we're spinning slowly, one of us will always be able to keep an eye on the action."

Pain kept the rotation going for two minutes before he set her down and gave her a hug. Two minutes of spinning could put anyone's equilibrium out of whack and he needed her support as much as she needed his to remain upright.

Several people applauded the impromptu performance as the ballet partners leaned into each other.

"What did you see?" he asked.

"I saw one of Graybeard's people summon Earnest Ernie and give a command."

"Ernie then approached a couple in the crowd who were very much enjoying the ballet and drew them off to the side."

Agony continued the narration. It was hard to take everything in when one was also focused on holding one's body as stiff as a board while being twirled in circles seven feet off the ground. "The couple at first looked very pissed off, but that didn't last too long. Ernie said something to them."

"And whatever he said turned their attitudes from one of irritation to one of plain old-fashioned fear and dread." Pain tried to surreptitiously shake the stress out of his arm muscles, not wanting his partner to know that she no longer had the weight of her six-year-old self and wasn't as easy to hold above his head for two solid minutes.

"Ernie led them out of the hall but not before they had given Graybeard a furtive glance," she added

"From what I saw at that point, they didn't look happy."

Agony agreed with the assessment. "They looked scared to death."

Having regained her sense of balance, she risked another glance at Graybeard. Sure enough, he was also looking at her. He gave her a quick smile and another wink before he escorted his cigar out of the hall.

She was tempted to go after him, which may or may not have been the wisest choice of actions, but she had to hold off. Several of Pain's groupies from the pool had arrived and wanted to drag him off to join the crowd that surrounded the stage and did their own erotic versions of Swan Lake.

With a possessive arm wrapped around his waist, she spun him away from the herd and guided him toward the door while she called to his admirers, "Sorry, ladies. Maybe tomorrow. Tonight, me and my man are going to our cottage to do little private dirty dancing. All of it will be available on the parting disc for your viewing pleasure once you get home. Wait until you see how creative he can get with his bolo."

Agony took a moment to look back at the frustrated vixens, licked her lips, and smiled.

"I thought she was Sheri and share alike." One of the frustrated vixens pouted.

"Not tonight she isn't. But tomorrow, my dears, is another day," answered another of the predators.

The gaggle giggled and began to make plans as they turned to find their next object of desire to help them enjoy the rest of the night.

"Thank you for that," Pain said once they were out of harm's way and almost at their cottage.

"Hey, what's a partner for?"

"I hate to say it, but Buchanan may be onto something. After seeing Graybeard and the terrified couple's reaction, there may be a third layer buried here."

"You mean something below the polished posh and unvarnished hedonism we have so far been treated to?"

They stepped around the now dry bag of useless electronics that was still outside their door and entered the cottage.

It had been a long day and Pain wanted to wrap it up. "There may very well be a third layer, where some very dangerous people form machinations for some dastardly shit while distracted revelers snort coke off someone else's wife's surgically uplifted breasts or behinds."

"That was an extremely convoluted sentence, but I understood every word of it." Agony looked at the clock. "I would say mañana but it already is. See ya in the morning."

"Sounds like a plan."

The morning dawned bright and clear. Did it ever dare to rain at the Moorfin? They suspected that not many people were early-risers while at the estate, so they decided to start by seeing if they could enjoy a quick breakfast at the Grab & Go. Thereafter, they would wander the grounds to see whatever daytime activities were available that weren't listed on the Moorfin's menu.

The Grab and Go did serve breakfast cafeteria-style, so the partners loaded their plates, chose a table, and enjoyed their first cup of coffee since their arrival. They expressed surprise that a couple of dozen guests were doing the same.

After he'd savored his first sip of the coffee and as he dug into his breakfast of eggs, toast, sausage, and hash browns, Pain offered an observation about their fellow diners.

"The crowd here seems more of the age to avail themselves of the early-bird specials at their local restaurants and then be in bed by nine."

"It's kind of refreshing after last night," Agony responded as she was about to start on her French toast.

"Look, hon, it's Dick and Sheri. Do you mind if we join you?"

They weren't afforded the time to politely decline the request as a man and woman set their plates down and joined them.

"John and Evelyn." The man made the introductions. "We met in the hot tub yesterday but never had a chance to get to know you."

"You seemed to be in rather a hurry to get back to your cottage," Evelyn added with a wink and a smile.

"Ahh, to be young again." John chuckled and stirred some powder into his coffee. The powder did not come from a small factory-produced packet but from a capsule he had snapped open. He dug in a pocket and offered a couple of capsules to their breakfast companions. "Help yourself. Nothing perks up a morning like a little orange."

Dick spoke for Sheri as he tried to politely decline the offer. "Thank you, but it's a little early yet for us to get started."

The man nodded, no offense taken, and handed one to Evelyn before he put the rest away.

His wife popped her capsule open and dumped it into her

cup. "There is orange juice and there is orange *juice*. Both of them have vitamin C, of course, but the capsule form takes the energy up several notches."

"I'm sure they do." Agony smiled. "So tell me, what does one do around here during the early parts of the day?"

The new arrivals looked at each other and John made the first response.

"Well, of course, there are the stables for the horse and hounds set, but I'm afraid you missed today's hunt. I think that today, quail was the goal, right, Evelyn?"

"Oh, the quail. Beautiful birds. And you should see how the chef cooks them on Quail Night. He has a secret sauce that is to die for."

"Especially if you are a quail." John laughed at his joke. "And of course there is always fishing at the lake."

"Is the lake stocked?" Pain was curious.

The man nodded. "Trout and bass, mostly. Freshwater fighting fish."

His wife smiled. "The pontoons are also well-stocked if you know what I mean. By the end of a fishing excursion, you won't care if you caught anything or not. There is nothing like a few fun hours out on the water."

That caught Pain's attention. "How often does a fishing excursion occur? And how many guests does a pontoon hold?"

John handled that question. "Each boat can hold a dozen and they leave from the dock every two hours on the hour. The even-numbered hours, that is."

"And, of course," Evelyn added, "if you prefer more gentle landlocked activities, there is always the Between the Legs Croquet Court."

"Between the legs croquet?" It was Sheri's turn to be curious.

The woman laughed again and explained. "The actual wickets are members of the club. They can hold their legs as close or far apart as they want—"

"And wear whatever they want while doing it." John seemed to feel that was important information.

His wife giggled and continued. "So the wickets can widen their legs or close them, depending on what kind of incentives the players offer."

John winked at the Moorfin virgins. "And the size of the mallets and the balls are totally up to the discretion of the players."

Dick checked his watch and stood. "Let's hurry, Sheri. A fishing pontoon is leaving in ten minutes. Thanks, guys."

He took his partner's hand, hurried her to the exit, and turned toward the dock.

Sheri waved a quick goodbye to their breakfast partners as she was dragged out. They walked at a brisk pace and were halfway to the dock before she asked, "Fishing?"

"We'll be in a confined space with a limited number of occupants and a shared goal. They can fish in the water, while we do our fishing onboard."

"Now and then, you make sense."

They caught the pontoon in time and hopped on board, only to discover that the other occupants were already hopped up.

They returned to their cottage later that afternoon with nothing more to show for their efforts than helping each other to fend off groping hands and politely declining the vast amount of candy that had been offered along the way.

Every time they had made any mention of Graybeard, someone immediately changed the subject. They were one pissed-off couple of undercover agents. Agony dug out the secure phone and called her report in.

"Tell me something good." Special Agent Second-Ring-Buchanan picked up immediately, as always.

"Well, the fish were biting but none of the guests were."

"So we have a second day of absolutely nothing?"

She became as defensive as she was annoyed. "Not absolutely nothing. We have discovered that no one wants to talk to us about Graybeard. We'll be having a friendly chat but if we bring him up by saying something as innocent as, 'Hey, we haven't had a chance to meet him yet, but who is the cigar man?' there is always a second of silence before someone changes the subject."

"But that is exactly what I need you two to find out. You are not on a pleasure cruise."

"We are not on a pleasure anything!" she snapped

"Then start working. Maybe they aren't talking to you because you're not selling yourselves hard enough as a couple."

"Pain has tossed me into a hot tub. He has thrown me over his shoulder and laughed while he announced to one and all that we needed some personal time. We have mingled at the ballet and accepted ass-grabs without breaking anyone's wrists and Pain seems to be rising high on the wish-list of dozens of women, half of them old enough to be his mother. Hell, he's fighting off more advances than I am."

"And still nothing?"

"If you want us to start collecting pharmaceutical candy samples, we could fill a suitcase. But when it comes to Graybeard? Yeah, we have nothing so far except a creepy vibe."

Buchanan's voice reflected everyone's mood. "Well, you'd better find something soon. Otherwise, you can forget a limo ride home and find your own way back."

With that, he ended the call.

"What does he want me to do? Blow Chief Chance simply to get some answers?" She stormed across the room and stashed the phone.

Pain echoed her frustration as he thrust the door to his bedroom open. "I'll go rinse off the fish-smell. You might want to do the same before we head to the Tantric Banquet that begins in four hours."

"The Tantric Banquet? Are you that desperate or are your groupies beginning to get you all hot and bothered?"

"I won't even respond to that." He disappeared into his bedroom at the same time another firm knock came from the door.

Agony yanked the door open and snapped, "What?"

Good old Chance stood there with a smile and waggling eyebrows and invited himself in. "Just who I was looking for."

She scowled and muttered under her breath, "I have to stop being the one to answer the door." Reluctantly, she closed the door before she called, "Honey? We have company!"

Pain's voice came from the other room. "Well, you can tell them to fuck off. We have all the Girl Scout cookies we need, so whatever they're selling, I'm not buying."

The chief managed to at least keep his pants on as he responded. "That works fine because it's only you I came looking for."

That announcement put her on high alert, but she remembered Buchanan's insistence and managed to put a light purr in her voice. "Oh, my. I'm flattered. What can little ol' me do for you, Chance?"

His lascivious grin was vomit-worthy. "Probably a lot, but that will have to wait for another time. I am here because Rolf has requested the pleasure of your company."

"Rolf?" She frowned at him.

"Hieronymous Rolf. He says you and he shared a moment across the room at the ballet last night and he would like to meet you. I am simply here to escort you. Nothing fancy, merely a quick hello. You will still have enough time to clean up and change before the banquet."

Pain had been listening from behind his door and decided to

put off his shower and step into the living room. "Only Sheri? Not me?"

"He didn't mention you, big guy." Chance shrugged but with no suggestion of an apology. "But don't worry. I'm sure your time will come."

The chief looked at Sheri as if he expected her to handle her man.

She had to take the opportunity. "It's okay, honey. You finish cleaning up while I go see Mr. Rolf. I'm sure that once I mention you, he'll invite you over too."

Her partner sounded skeptical. "Yeah, I'm sure he will." He flashed her a warning look to be careful. "You know, I think I might go hang out at the pool until you get back."

Chance nodded and smiled at that suggestion. "One can never get too much time in at the pool."

Pain watched his partner being escorted up the trail to the main lodge. He changed into his pool attire, reasoning that it was right up against the side of the lodge and therefore much closer to where Agony would be than the cottage should something go wrong. Since nothing had gone right yet, he thought it would be the best option.

CHAPTER FOURTEEN

The chief seemed to be in a congenial mood as he walked beside Agony toward the lodge.

"I'm telling you, Sheri, it usually takes several visits for Mr. Rolf to take an interest in anyone, but you have caught his attention in less than two full days on your initial stay."

She tried to smile and play along. "It must be my perfume. The commercials all said that it was simply irresistible. Maybe for once, there was some truth in advertising."

"We'll have to ask Mr.Rolf which of his five senses you seem to have so captivated. Me? I'm an eye kind of guy."

After that comment, she made sure that they climbed the stairs side by side. No way would she give him a clear view of her ass as he led her up a staircase that ended on the roof of the four-story lodge and opened into a solarium.

The glassed-domed enclosure had enough lounge chairs to easily hold a dozen sun-bathers but at that time, the only occupants were Graybeard and his cigar. The chief made the introductions.

"Mister Hieronymous Rolf, I am pleased to present Sheri, who has also expressed interest in meeting you."

"Have you now, my dear?"

Agony responded with a half-smile and a half-bow. "Well, you do have a very distinguished presence, although I must admit that I am more interested in you than your choice of Havana's finest."

"Ahh, yes." Graybeard regarded his cigar and regretfully but with proper etiquette, set it aside to smolder.

Having made the introductions, Police Chief Chauncey Morris respectfully took a couple of steps back.

Mr. Rolf stood, took her hand, and guided her to a chair next to his.

"I find the late afternoon sun to be the most pleasant. Mid-afternoon is often too bright, and the morning? Well, in my younger days, I used to welcome each morning's sun in but now? Perhaps it is because I am advancing in years but I prefer the close of the day. In the morning, especially if one is young, one can become excited about what new adventures await each day, but I have had enough of adventures. Now, I prefer to look back on each day and reflect on all that has come to pass. Does that mean, Ms. Sheri, that I am getting old?"

"No, Mr. Rolf. That means that you are gathering wisdom and taking the time to reflect."

"Well put. Very well put. Have you enjoyed your first visit to the lodge?"

She tried to answer that honestly. "There is so much to take in that I'm more overwhelmed than relaxed. Maybe by my next visit, I will be more able to enjoy it than to worry about how I am presenting myself to all the other guests."

Hieronymous nodded. "Yes, yes, quite understandable. Most are quite privileged and fortunate to be in the positions they occupy. I find that group to be rather tedious and, if I may say so, boring. I much prefer the company of the ruthless and ambitious—the ones who, from various backgrounds, have fought to rise above and separate themselves from the mundane and stake their territory."

Agony thought she might finally be making some headway. "And how would you describe those people? Ruthless? Predatory? Determined?"

"All three, I suppose. One thing they never are is boring. I simply cannot abide boring, which is why you caught my attention. I use the lodge as a way to separate the wheat from the chaff. The chaff, I leave to go on their inconsequential way. But the wheat? Ahh, the wheat. Those are the ones I often gather into my inner circle."

She showed the appropriate amount of respect as she asked, "I imagine that your inner circle has more important considerations than partying the night away while at a lodge?"

"Precisely. Power is not found in the nearest pool. That is one of the reasons why, the first time I saw you, I thought you and your associate might be a perfect fit."

Agony was so excited about finally making some progress that she completely missed the use of the word associate as opposed to husband.

Mr. Rolf continued. "My cursory glance at Sheri and Dick's backgrounds suggested that you would be the kind of power-couple I would love to bring in—rich and ruthless. When I met your gaze at the ballet last night, I felt confirmation. That is why I asked my staff to dig a little deeper because one's instincts must always be balanced by reality, wouldn't you agree?"

She nodded in agreement. "Appearances can often be deceiving."

It was a little discomforting that with only one look in her eye, she could be judged as such a predator that Hieronymous Rolf felt a kinship with her. She reassured herself that maybe she had successfully pulled off her Sheri act.

Mr. Rolf's face took on a note of sadness. "So you can understand my disappointment when I discovered that you and Pain, first initial M, were operating under fabricated aliases."

Oh shit!

Not at all happy that his partner was in the lion's den without him, Pain hurried to the pool. Once there, he located the balcony where Graybeard had sat and observed the day before, determined to keep an eye out for any distress signal Agony might put out.

The trolley cart of goodies was about to depart but he caught it in time to be able to get a plastic cup of iced coffee. He was about to search for a deck chair that would allow him a clear view of the balcony when he realized he was in the clutches of three of the women who had seemed so enamored with him the afternoon before.

"Well, hello, Dickie-Doodle." A hand grasped his right arm. "We barely had the time to introduce ourselves yesterday, but I'm Crystal."

"And I'm Jenny." His left arm was also firmly grasped as the second of the three introduced herself.

"And I am Marci," the third said as they guided him to their table where he had little choice but to take a seat unless he wanted to cause a major disturbance.

"Do you mind if I take this chair?" he asked and chose the one facing Graybeard's balcony.

Crystal giggled her response. "Your derriere, your choice of chairs."

He noticed that the table was located almost directly under the balconies of one of the lodge's three wings that edged the pool and only had about six feet of space between the wing and the water. The balconies protruded far enough that one would have to stand on the edge of them to even be able to see the pool.

"Marci and I," Jenny explained, "have a suite on the third floor directly above us. That makes it easy for us to drop things down to each other in case an emergency arises."

"An emergency?" He wasn't sure what would qualify as an emergency at the poolside.

Marci laughed. "Oh, you know…things like missing the trolley or maybe needing a new top because the one you had worn had somehow ended up being used in a game of keep-away and got torn when the game got a little rambunctious. Little things like that."

"You should see the view from their balcony," Crystal added.

"Yes," Jenny agreed, "you should."

No, Pain thought, *I really shouldn't,* but he laughed playfully, sipped his iced coffee, and kept most of his focus on Graybeard's balcony. Later, he realized that he should probably have kept a closer eye on his drink.

"The identities were fabricated perfectly." Hieronymous Rolf retrieved his cigar, took a leisurely puff, and enjoyed his feeling of power. "Those were not an issue, per se. Who doesn't want to present themselves as someone else now and then, especially at the Moorfin?"

That comment drew a brief cough from the police chief. Rolf caught the hint to move it along.

"The only thing that caught my attention was a fingerprint left on one of the identifications. A fingerprint that belonged to neither you nor Mr. Pain."

"And who did it belong to?" Agony tried to look confused and hoped it could all be explained although her first guess was her least favorite FBI Special Agent.

"A low-level FBI employee who was probably the one assigned the duties but who failed to wipe the card clean before handing it over. And that, of course, inspired us to run you and your partner's fingerprints."

So not Buchanan. We were busted by a careless technician.

Graybeard leaned back in his chair and savored his moment. "As long as one has the money, the game of make-believe is perfectly acceptable at the Moorfin. What is not acceptable is inviting the FBI to join the game." He took another puff. "I do truly hope that you, Alicia Goni, and Pain, first initial M, have enjoyed your visit to our humble lodge. Sadly, you will not live long enough to finish your stay."

Police chief Chauncey Morris's footfalls were not as light as he imagined them to be as he came up behind her. Agony tipped her chair back and into his legs, and he tumbled over both her and the chair, a garrote in his hands.

He had the weight advantage but she had speed and agility on her side and delivered a knee to his crotch before she rolled out from under him as they both landed heavily. A quick baton-strike to the side of his head turned his lights out for the immediate future and she scrambled to her feet. She fully expected to find Hieronymous Rolf chuckling as he took another puff, pointed a gun calmly at her, and fired.

Instead, she confronted a terrified old man standing in a position that seemed to scream, "What have you done?"

She didn't have time to process what that meant before two security personnel rushed in through the solarium's door. They paused to take in the scene but she acted immediately. With one quick foot-first leap, she crushed one of the intruder's windpipe and with her baton, broke the wrist of the one who had managed to draw a gun.

The weapon went off, but the bullet had been aimed where she had been, not where she now was. Another whack of her baton made solid contact with his head and put the second intruder down.

She spun in Hieronymous Rolf's direction and still expected

him to fire at her. Instead, he clutched his throat and tried to stem the blood from the bullet wound that one of his two security guards had inadvertently delivered.

The last words he heard as he tried to draw his last breath were from the woman who was the last one standing in the room. "Go ahead and try to fingerprint the bullet, creep! I can guarantee you that my prints won't be on it."

With their cover blown, she had to find Pain as quickly as possible because his life was no doubt also in danger. *Pool,* she remembered him saying. *He would head to the pool.*

She left the bodies to sort themselves out and ran down the flights of stairs, reluctant to take the time to wait for an elevator. Once on the ground floor, she rushed out to the pool area where she found her partner.

If she was swept into a witness box and sworn-in to tell the truth, the whole truth, and nothing but the truth, and was asked, "How did you feel about your partner at that moment?" her response would have been, "Partner? Who is this partner you speak of?"

After all that she had gone through in the solarium, the last thing she needed or expected to see was him naked and taking a swan-dive from a third-floor balcony into what she hoped was the deep end of the pool. Although if it had been into the shallow end and he broke his neck...well, if she was still under oath at that moment, she wouldn't have shed any tears.

She elbowed through the poolside crowd who applauded Pain's dive wildly and called, "He knows how to dive but he doesn't know how to swim! A little help here?"

Several women would have been glad to help but they all seemed to settle at the edge of the pool in case mouth-to-mouth resuscitation was necessary. It took four men to help Pain out of the pool and into her arms.

"Thanks, guys!" She addressed her man's rescuers with what she hoped was credible gratitude and decided to add a little misdirection. "We'll be in cottage number six if anyone wants to drop by for a nightcap."

Agony looped one of Pain's arms over her shoulders, helped him out of the pool area, and tried to hurry him to their cottage before all kinds of alarms could sound.

"That was fun," he mumbled as he stumbled alongside her.

"What was fun?" She struggled under his weight.

"Umm...something. I'm sure that something was fun."

She managed to get his big naked ass back to and inside cottage number four, dropped him face down on the floor, and hoped she could undo some of the damage as she scrambled for the flip phone. She pressed redial and lodged the phone between her ear and shoulder as she leapt onto her partner and pressed hard on the back of his chest in rhythmic beats with both hands.

Buchanan answered at the same time that Pain puked. Fortunately, the vomit was of the projectile kind and landed a foot away and in front of his head.

"I'll call you back!" She slid the phone into a pocket, rolled off her partner, and helped him into a seated position against the closest chair she could find.

"Stay!" she commanded as she pressed redial. "Die!" she responded when Buchanan answered on the first ring.

"Is there a problem?" The agent remained calm, reasoning that at least one of them had to.

"Yeah, there's a fucking problem. Your techie left a fingerprint on one of our ID packets and the entire lodge force will swarm after us at any second."

"What about Mr. Graybeard?"

"Graybeard's name is—correct that, was—Hieronymous Rolf."

"Was?"

"Yeah, was," she confirmed acidly. "But not by my hands."

"Pain's?" He sounded worried.

"No, not his either. He was too busy being drugged by pool party patrons."

She could hear Buchanan pound some keys. "I'm not pulling anything up regarding a Hieronymous Rolf."

"Well, that's the name he gave me."

"I think I might be able to stand now," Pain said as he tried and fell to his knees, his hands placed firmly on the floor in an effort not to French-kiss the carpet.

The agent remained calm. It was easy to do when you were on the other end of the call. "Mr. Rolf doesn't show up anywhere in my databases so it must be a false name. His whole existence might be fabricated."

"You think?" Agony kept the phone perched on her shoulder as she tried to heft Pain onto his feet and walk his naked ass around the room. She managed to snatch one bottle of water from the fridge and toss the contents into his face before she retrieved another and forced him to drink it. Her tactics were a little rough but she had to get him dressed and ambulatory as quickly as possible.

"We missed the shadow!" Buchanan suddenly sounded excited.

"Say again?" She didn't have time for guessing games. The lodge's security forces were sure to be out in large numbers at any second.

"Where is Clark Kent when Superman makes an appearance? Where is Bruce Wayne when Batman shows up?"

It wasn't enough for her to have to deal with a drugged-up Pain. She now had to deal with an FBI agent who might have taken too many trips around the bend and was in danger of losing his grasp on coherency forever.

"Graybeard was only the face!" Buchanan slowed his speech to become comprehensible. "He wasn't Clark and Superman any more than he was Batman and Bruce Wayne. Someone had to stand in the shadows the whole time to keep an eye on things and pull the strings. Think, Agony, think! Who was always within sight whenever Graybeard was around?"

"Oh, fuck!" she exclaimed and went silent as she replayed every scene since their arrival in her head.

The agent seemed to follow the process or at least make the same deduction. "My guess is that the city's chief of police has always been there, somewhere in the background, whenever you have seen Hieronymous Rolf?"

"Every single time. The man seems to be omnipresent and acts the part of the powerful buffoon."

"Chalk one up for him."

"I'm glad we got that resolved." Agony still had a naked and half-befuddled Pain on her hands. "So what's our next move?"

A short pause was followed by a sincerely unapologetic apology from Special Agent Marshal Buchanan. "My next move is to thank you for giving me all the information I needed to proceed. Your next move is to try to get yourselves out of there alive. But that, I am afraid, is not something I can help you with. This one is too far off the books for me to pull in any assistance on, but I'm sure that you two will be able to find a way out of it."

The phone went dead.

Agony looked at her partner, who was still naked but at least now able to stand on his own two feet without too much help.

"Get dressed!" she ordered.

He was considerably less befuddled than he had been before he'd vomited but wasn't yet in full fighting form.

"Will khaki's be okay for the occasion?"

"Yes! Khaki's will be fine. And don't forget your cowboy boots."

"Okay, then. I love those boots."

Pain did his best to hurry to his room and change while she cursed Buchanan and listened for the sound of security forces rushing toward their cottage.

She changed hastily as well into long pants, a t-shirt, and a jacket before she slipped every weapon she could find into her ensemble. It was time to make a run for it.

CHAPTER FIFTEEN

Making a stumble for it may have been a more accurate phrase than making a run for it, but things were what they were. The partners managed to get out of the cottage a few minutes before the security forces arrived.

They had escaped the cottage but there wasn't much in the way of cover other than a few barbecue pits and a handful of trees. Pain was steady enough to do a slow jog but was not up to fighting mode yet. A shot rang out to let them know they had been seen.

"Do you think you can reach the stables on your own?" Agony pulled out two of her guns.

"I think so. There is a wide path to them through the woods and it comes out on this end a little ahead and to the left."

"Right."

"Oh, to the right?" He realized that his head might still be more muddled than he thought.

"No, I meant, correct. The path is up ahead toward the left. You make a run for it. I'll try to slow them and catch up with you."

It wasn't in his nature to run but she gave him a shove and he complied as quickly as he could, hoping that the adrenaline would kick in soon.

There seemed to be only half a dozen pursuers for now. No one knew she was armed so they ran at her full-speed and fired wildly. They also moved as a group instead of fanning out, so she took a stance and fired at the center. A scream made the group pause long enough for her to be able to scramble behind a tree.

When she peered out, the group had now split into two. She fired three shots into each group, heard another scream, and began to run. She caught up with Pain halfway to the stables where he had stopped and was waiting for her. He had a touch of blood on his cheek but it looked like the result of a branch scratch.

"Why aren't you moving?" she screamed as she approached him. "Are you going comatose on me again?"

He shook his head. "No, I'm fine. Most of the cobwebs are gone. How many and how far behind?"

"Two fewer than there were, so maybe only four. I think they stopped the immediate pursuit. Me having weapons threw them off. But I'm sure they'll call reinforcements in so we gotta get moving."

"I can move."

"Remember, you don't have your magical Underoos. They're in Bertha so you are mortal now."

They rushed onward to the stables.

The hunt master had what he thought was a perfect gig—a comfortable cottage, horses, ATVs, and guns. What more could an outdoorsman want? When he heard gunfire in the distance, he made a quick inventory of the weapons that had been left in his care. Every one of the guns was present and accounted for, so he grabbed a shotgun and headed out to see what all the commotion was about.

The commotion caught him head-on as Pain bull-rushed him before he even had a chance to aim and fire. He snatched the shotgun out of the hunt master's hands and used the butt-end to knock him out and down. Agony was relieved to see that her partner was finally returning to normal.

She rushed into the cottage and found that the case holding the weapons had been left open. Without hesitation, she snagged as many as she could and tossed them into a canvas carry bag.

"Save some for me," Pain told her as he followed her in.

He approached the case and took stock. Knowing him, she was surprised when he chose a couple of double-barreled shotguns whose straps let him sling them over his shoulders. He also chose two short, fat pistols. If they hadn't been in such a rush, she would have recognized them for what they were but given the situation they were in, she didn't waste any time asking questions.

He shrugged when he saw her expression. "My no guns rule is more of a preference than a policy. Let's find some rides."

They raced to the covered carport where the ATVs and dirt bikes were parked, but the keys must have been kept in the cottage. Pain could hot-wire a car but had no experience with ATVs and had always been too large for the standard dirt bike. They heard the security forces approaching fast. From the shouts, the reinforcements had caught up with the original team and he guessed there were about two dozen of them by now.

Agony caught his arm. "The stables and the horses! You know how to ride a horse, right?"

"I've had more experience with camels, but yeah. I know which end bites and which end kicks."

He helped himself to a couple of two-gallon red plastic cans, ripped his belt off, strung them together, and held them as he ran.

Once in the stable, they hefted saddles onto the closest two horses they could find. She chose a lovely tan-and-white mare. He was left with a large black stallion and he slung the red cans on the back of the saddle. They guided the steeds out the door and galloped through the clearing toward the woods as shots rang out.

"Do you have any idea where to go?" she shouted.

"In the opposite direction from the guns firing at us!" he suggested reasonably.

As they hadn't had time to join any of the hunts yet, all they could do was guess which path to take. The sound of the ATVs springing to life and beginning to roar after them didn't allow much time for decision-making, so Pain let Agony lead and they both hoped for the best.

She tried to use the fallback habit of when in doubt, go north, but the denseness of the trees made it hard to tell which direction the setting sun was in.

"I'm a little fuzzy on what happened," he told her as they stopped at a small space where four paths intersected. "How did they make us?"

"One of Buchanan's finest left a fingerprint on one of our IDs." She had to fight a little to keep her spirited mare under control, but she leaned forward over her neck and finger-flipped her ear. When the horse looked back at her, she gave her a couple of carrots she had snatched from a bag of equine treats. She now had a new best girlfriend. "They traced the print to the FBI and I don't know how, but from there, they were able to ID both of us."

"Someone at the Moorfin has deep connections."

"My best guess right now is that it's Chauncey Morris. He tried to garrote me. Garrote me!" Her voice rose a little in indignation.

"Did you kill him?"

"No, but he'll need more than a handful of aspirin when he comes to. And Graybeard died a scared old man when one of his security officers fired a shot that went off course."

"What do you think the chances are that Buchanan's ID expert was ordered to intentionally leave a fingerprint?" he asked after a moment's thought.

"Woah, woah!" He wasn't sure if his partner was talking to him or her horse. She cleared that up with her next sentence. "That would mean Buchanan set us up."

Pain nodded. "He set us up to gather the information he needed and not have to worry about extracting us. We were the perfect patsies."

"I sincerely hope you are wrong about that."

"Why?"

"Because I don't want my epitaph to read, *Died by her own stupidity.*"

The engines roared closer.

"You need to choose a path here," he reminded her

She frowned as she scanned the three paths leading out. "Rock, paper, scissors. You win, we go right. I win, we go left."

"What about straight ahead?"

"Okay." She resisted a sigh. "If it's a tie, we go straight."

"Works for me."

Pain went with paper. Agony went with scissors and they spurred their horses down the left-hand path.

"Let's go, girl." She patted her mare's neck.

At first, the path sloped downward gradually but eventually began to ascend in a slightly curving course.

He followed again as she took the lead and shouted as quietly as he could, "If they realize which path we took, they might split up. Half of them will follow while the other half take shortcuts to where the path ends so they can wait in ambush."

"Are you always this cheerful while being pursued?" She spurred her horse down the path as quickly as she could and trusted that the animal knew the way better than she did.

"Call me an optimist," he retorted. "Two halves of an enemy force, one behind and one ahead, is a damn sight better than the entire force at the same place. Someone has to get to the end of this trail first so let's make sure it's us."

From the sound of the engines, they knew that at least some of the forces in pursuit were indeed following them on the trail. As Agony directed their course, Pain unscrewed one of the caps on the red plastic cans and leaned back as far as he could, held it out, and let it drain behind him. The can now empty, he tossed it aside and paused.

She sensed him stop, reined her horse quickly, and turned to face him.

"I won't leave you alone to fight half the brigade," she protested

He held up one of the pistols she hadn't had the time to identify yet. "Who said I'm going to fight? When in need of help, it's always a good idea to have a flare-gun handy."

Pain aimed the pistol at the end of the gasoline trail the red plastic can had left and fired.

The flame of the flare caught the near end of it and the last hundred yards of the trail they had traveled through burst into flames.

"I merely gave them a cause to pause," he explained. "Can we get our move-groove on again?"

That was all she needed to hear and she turned, leaned over her horse's neck, and informed her mare, "It's time for us girls to show all those stupid boys how it's done." Ms. Tan-and-White seemed happy to oblige.

Horses were used to taking commands, especially if they had been raised at the Moorfin and had spent most of their time taking orders from the two-legged weekend warriors who would pull too hard on the reins and make demands from what they assumed were stupid four-legged creatures that possessed neither gas pedals nor steering wheels.

Agony's mare surged into a gallop. Pain's steed knew enough to follow the leader and he knew enough to hold on for dear life and keep his head as close to his horse's neck as possible. The two horses raced up the path and didn't seem to care if their riders took an overhanging branch or two in their faces.

The path brought them to an open field with the sun directly ahead and about half an hour from setting. Three sides of the field, including the one they had merged from, were surrounded by woods. Once in the clearing, they reined their horses in to get their bearings.

The sound of engines and shots ringing out from one of the corners of the field confirmed that there had indeed been a shortcut that part of the security patrol they were trying to elude had known about. But those engines and shots came from their side and slightly behind, not from ahead.

"If you say, 'Hi ho, Silver, away,'" Agony promised, "I will put a bullet through your head myself."

"How about, run like the wind, faithful steeds?"

"That, I can live with."

No further discussion of plans was necessary and the partners used their heels to gently spur their faithful mare and stallion on as they raced forward across the flat open ground. Each of the horses seemed to enjoy the freedom to be able to stretch their legs for a change.

The roar of engines followed. Some came from the corner where the ambush had been set up and a little later, a few from directly behind once they had navigated through the fire Pain had left.

It was never a fair chase. Even if the field went on forever, the horses would have eventually run out of energy long before the ATVs and dirt bikes had run out of gas. Dozens of wild shots rang out from behind and their pursuers seemed to be having a grand old time.

As part of the security force, most of their duties involved breaking up minor squabbles and helping drunk guests to their rooms to sleep it off. They would often join the hunts because at least they allowed them to shoot at something, and they always kept track of who had scored the most kill-shots. Now, suddenly, they had actual human prey to track and bring in with extreme force.

In spite of the fact that most of the Moorfin's guests considered the security force as a group of lightweight rent-a-cops, they were all ex-military collecting easy paychecks. But collecting a weekly check for doing little more than next to nothing didn't mean they weren't still hungry for some real action. The latest call to arms had more than a little bloodlust running through some veins.

Shots were fired wildly from a distance behind their quarry.

The only thing that stopped the horses was a cliff that the partners didn't know existed. If they'd had the time to study the aerial photos Buchanan had shown them, they would have known that the Gaughan River sliced through part of the Moorhpin's property.

A section of the property met the river on the lower ground, where canoes and raft trips were often used as a starting point for mild river excursions. Where they were now, however, they looked down at the flowing water from the top of a fifty-foot sheer drop-off cliff.

"It's too steep for us to walk the horses down." Agony judged the odds, which were not in their favor.

"And the water's probably too shallow for us to not break our bones jumping into it."

They were about to discuss their options when a bullet ripped through her left arm. She cried out and tumbled from her horse.

"Where are you hit?" Pain was ready to dismount, sweep her into his arms, and slide down the cliff and into the water if that was what was needed to save her.

"Only my arm but it might have chipped a bone. It's hellishly painful but no major artery was touched."

"Don't move! I'll be right back," he ordered and she grimaced.

"You'd better be. Otherwise, I will write you out of my will."

"If you die, do I get Bertha?" She wasn't entirely sure if his question was a joke or not.

"Only in your dreams," she retorted to play it safe.

That was all he needed to hear.

"Game on, assholes!" He flashed her a final glance before he swung his steed and galloped full-speed ahead into the noisy crowd of pursuers.

From her cop days, she knew how to bandage a wound quickly, whether it was her own or a victim's. In those situations, she would wait for an EMS driver to appear and do a more professional job while they performed triage before they headed to a hospital, sometimes with sirens blaring and sometimes not.

Some injuries were simply flesh wounds and there was no rush. Other wounds were much more deadly and the ambulance would race away, red lights be damned. When it came to the worst wounds…well, there was no need for an ambulance to rush. All they had to do was transport a dead body to the morgue for an autopsy and no one needed a siren for that.

She did a decent job and managed to staunch her blood flow. That done, she stood, held onto her tan-and-white mare that had kept her from rushing headlong over a cliff, and whispered calming words into her ear while she watched her partner in action in a way she had never seen him before.

Agony realized that Pain had the bright setting sun at his back. This meant it was in his attacker's eyes, which was never a bad strategy.

He rode his black horse at a headlong pace toward their pursuers as he took hold of a loop attached to the second red plastic can, swung it three times over his head, and let it fly. While it was still in mid-air and descending over the first of the motorized vehicle riders, he pulled out the second of his flare-guns and fired.

The gas can burst into flames and fire fell from the sky. None of the Moorfin's security forces had thought to don flame-retardant suits and half of them fell off their ATVs and dirt bikes. They scrambled to put each other's fires out as their gas-powered vehicles began to erupt into flames around them.

Pain wasted no time with politeness. He leapt off his black stallion and slapped him to send him running off and out of harm's way.

With the horse now safe, he had the two shotguns he'd borrowed from the hunt master. He fired one at the first three of the ATV riders to find their feet and the other in the opposite direction, hoping to hit any stationary target.

Two other men rose out of the carnage and the flames that were now a massive blaze. He eliminated both, threw his now empty shotguns aside, and strode into the smoke to snatch up any gun the possessor of which would no longer need.

Shots erupted from all directions in the inferno as ATVs and motorbikes continued to burst into flames and spew black smoke into the air.

All Agony could make out was the image of a large man who rushed and rolled through the smoke and the flames, firing shots from weapons he must have picked up along the way. The huge shadow stood on the far side of the inferno in the field for a moment and a fusillade of shots was unleashed at him from a dozen different angles.

He continued to run, duck, roll, and fire. A dozen or so ATVs rampaged in circles but one of them was now being driven by Pain. He had ripped a strip of cloth from one of the dead attacker's sleeves and tied it tightly around the gas handle of the vehicle. This allowed him to drive at top speed and steer with one hand while he used his other hand to wreak havoc with the submachine guns he had claimed.

The opposing ATVs were occupied by pairs, one driving and the other riding behind and firing. He mostly aimed for the riders first and the gas tanks second. Hundreds of shots were fired, followed by hundreds more in response. Bodies, on fire from the leakage of the gas tanks that ignited, would run and try to roll the flames out. He put most of them out of their misery with a few quick bursts.

The dozen dirt bikes were another issue. Each one had only one rider and would have to stop and fire. It was hard for him to tell where his targets were through the smoke, but whenever he heard a bike stop, he fired several bursts at the point of silence. More often than not, his volleys resulted in screams.

Through the haze, Pain could make out three or four remaining ATVs grouped together, no doubt trying to plan their next course of action. He spun his in a quick circle and aimed directly for the small group. Clearing the smoke and knowing that he had the vehicle aimed correctly, he leapt off, rolled, and let loose with all the rounds he had left as it crashed into the circle and burst into flames.

Pain snatched up another sub that someone had carelessly left behind and picked off the half-dozen survivors. As he walked through the carnage, he found a couple of AKs, collected them, and hurried in his partner's direction.

Agony saw him emerge from the chaos as flames continued to rise behind him. He had looked better but never scarier.

"Please don't ask me for a body count," he said shortly.

"Why is that?" She wondered if it was wise to ask

"Because it wasn't a fair fight. How bad is your arm?"

"It needs tending to," she responded and she meant every word.

"If I help you onto your mare, do you think she has enough strength to return through the woods to the lodge?"

"Will she have to carry you too?"

"No." He shook his head. "I think I left one dirt bike still functional."

She frowned. "You think?"

"I don't know. There were so many guns going off back there. Hang on."

Pain disappeared for a moment and returned dragging a dirt bike. Its deceased rider still had a boot tangled in its handlebars.

"He tried to get off a trick shot," he explained bluntly.

She made no comment and he untangled the boot and its rider from the bike and helped her onto her horse. They left the carnage behind and he followed her and her mare as they hurried to the lodge area.

Once there, he helped her off her faithful horse and together, they made a wide circle around the pool area where the evening party was just getting into gear and stepped into the parking lot, where he hot-wired a Lexus sedan.

"We're stealing a car?" she asked as he helped her into the passenger seat, worried about her wound.

"It seems like the perfect end to a perfect day. No lodge sirens are going off and all the gunfire has probably already been written off to a fireworks display that someone forgot to mention as one of tonight's activities. It will probably take at least three days before whoever owns this knows that it's missing. Would you rather I steal a Toyota?"

"How's the gas?" She chose not to answer what was a stupid question.

"Almost a full tank."

That was all she needed to know.

"Then please, get us the fuck out of here."

Pain complied and drove to the cottage, threw their suitcases in, and accelerated to the gate. His priority was to get her arm tended to.

Wounded but not in any danger of dying, she closed her eyes and trusted her partner to have a destination in mind where she could be treated and bandaged.

She would have liked to have been able to sleep, but in spite of all of the betrayals they had experienced while at the Moorfin, all she could see behind her closed lids was her partner spewing death in the clearing with a handful of guns in his hands and coming out of it as if... As if what?

Merely another day at the office? No, that wasn't right. He had come out of it looking like he didn't want to be a man who could leave so much destruction in his wake, no matter how well-deserved it had been.

Whether it was from the loss of blood or the pain from the bullet having nicked a bone, she finally passed out. Her last thoughts were of Pain saying, *Don't make me angry. You won't like me when I'm angry,* before he turned green and held a dozen weapons in each hand.

CHAPTER SIXTEEN

It was a two-hour drive to the city. Agony's arm needed serious attention, but since the injury had come from a bullet wound, an emergency room visit at a hospital would have caused too many complications. Doctors didn't like bullet wounds. Nor did the police who they would have been legally obligated to call in.

The partners had enough questions of their own at the moment and were in no mood to answer more coming from the boys in blue network. At Pain's suggestion, she opened the Lexus' glove compartment and found travel-sized bottles of pain killers and ED pills. With her good arm, she managed to retrieve a bottle of Motrin and dry-swallowed a couple.

He was torn between wanting her to be able to rest but remain conscious and talking so he could judge how much blood she had lost by how coherent she was. He mostly chose to let her rest but would ask an innocuous question every half-hour or so as a gauge.

"Who the hell cares if *Die Hard* is considered a Christmas movie or not? Are you trying to keep me awake, or piss me off with stupid questions?" she demanded belligerently.

"Either one works."

She shook her head. The Motrin had helped but her arm still hurt like hell and she wasn't in the mood for movie trivia. "You haven't told me where we're headed yet."

"We'll drop in on a couple of old friends."

"At this hour? With a gunshot wound? Who the hell are we—oh, no, you're taking me to visit Iggy?"

"Who better to patch up a bullet wound in the middle of the night? Besides, Miles has a computer and I need to do some quick research."

She closed her eyes and leaned back. Miles and Ignatius's Funeral Home was run by two once upstanding citizens. Douglas Miles was a pharmacist who had become a little too addicted to some of the meds he dispensed. He lost his license but not his connections.

Jules Ignatius was a former coroner for the city but had a weakness for betting on the ponies. This weakness landed him in some serious trouble when some of his creditors had shown up and he had to make a few shady deals to get himself out of debt. It cost him his job and a two-year suspension of his medical license.

The dysfunctional duo had managed to find each other and with what they had left, scraped up enough to go into business as a funeral home, minimum licensing needed. Their establishment would never appear on anyone's top-ten list of high-end funeral parlors, but if you needed late-night, off-the-books surgery or a stash of high-grade street drugs, they had become the go-to guys.

Pain pulled the borrowed Lexus into the parking lot shortly after midnight. This was still early for Jules Ingatius, who usually had the majority of his wounded clients arrive after the bars and clubs had served last-call. If anyone in the city heard late-night gunfire and no police were called, the chances were good that the participants were headed to see Iggy.

Agony was weaker from the loss of blood than she had let on and he had to carry her to the door in his arms and kick on it until it was answered by Iggy himself. The funeral home didn't keep an overnight receptionist on staff.

The ex-coroner was shocked to find them on his doorstep with one of them wounded. "You are supposed to show up to bust me, not as one of the busted."

"What can I say? It's been a strange day." Pain pushed past him and headed to Iggy's makeshift surgical theater.

"It's a little early, isn't it?" Miles complained as he stuck his head out of his office and immediately regretted it.

"Don't go too far, Miles," he responded. "And close the porn sites. I will need your computer."

The man retreated hastily into his office and launched into action. He was much more concerned about hiding his inventory of pharmaceuticals than clearing his browser's history. The ex-agent could do serious damage to someone's stock when provoked.

Ignatius hurried around and ahead of Pain and held the door open as he carried Agony in and set her down on a table.

"I don't think I need to tell you the level of priority care that this patient will receive." His dead-eye stare matched the seriousness of his tone.

"No. You don't."

"Because otherwise, I'll leave here with one of your discount coffins. Have you ever seen the scratches inside a coffin from an occupant who was buried alive in one?"

"Message received." Iggy took a step back and studied them for a moment.

Pain seemed to have a few scratches, but his clothes had taken a beating. Both he and the garments were covered in ashes and reeked of smoke that could only be found in fires, not in a room of brandy and fine cigars.

Agony was much cleaner, except for her roughly bandaged and bleeding arm. He quickly and expertly cut her sleeve off and unwrapped the bandages.

"She says the bullet might have nicked a bone."

"I was about to tell him that myself." It was embarrassing enough to find herself under the care of Jules Ignatius but it was another thing to feel like she also had a babysitter. "How about you toodle along now and play nice with Miles and his computer and see what you can come up with?"

"Well, at least her spirits are still in good shape," Ignatius observed.

Pain hovered long enough to watch the doctor retrieve a cart loaded with antiseptic wipes, bottles, and various delicate surgical implements. He cleaned the wound, made a quick inspection, and inserted a thin pair of what looked like tweezers into the open gash.

"Does this hurt?" he asked mildly.

A quick right to his jaw was her answer.

Her partner decided that the doctor was closer to death than she was and wandered off to track Miles down.

Pain located the office and gave Miles the courtesy of knocking before he barged in. The door opened quickly and his first thought was that the man had been a little careless with the lines of powder he had been sniffing. There was more white powder around his lips than there was on his nose.

He had also gained thirty of the sixty pounds he had lost between the time Pain first met him and the second visit. The white and orange box open on the desk helped to explain both mysteries. It seemed that Douglas Miles had added donuts covered in powdered sugar to his list of addictions.

"Your office is a mess." He pointed out the obvious.

"Yeah, well. Things can go to hell fast when you lose your office assistant," Miles said morosely.

On their last visit, the partners had met Silvia, his twenty-year-old—at the most—administrative assistant, who was so proud of having been given a desk of her own. They didn't like to think about what Silvia had done to earn it but suspected one of the things was her talent for doing what she could under Miles' desk.

Her pay was probably minimum wage, but one of the fringe benefits was being able to join her boss as they indulged in testing the inventory.

"No more Silvia?"

"We don't mention her name around here, thank you very much." The man sighed, sat, and helped himself to another donut. "Ahh, hell. I may as well tell you. If I don't, I'll have to listen to Jules' version again, complete with his cackling. There was a Rap-off or something at a late-night club. A couple of the rappers took the competition a little too seriously and ended up in the back alley shooting it out with each other. Sadly, they were both terrible shots."

"Someone else got hurt by a stray bullet?" Pain didn't like the story very much thus far.

"No, unfortunately. If that had been the case, I would still have an administrative assistant. All they managed to do was graze each other, which is how they both ended up seeking Jules out. Long story short, she whose name is not mentioned fell in love with one of them and turned in her resignation on the spot."

"It's hard for an old man to compete with an up-and-coming superstar." He tried but failed to keep the sarcasm out of his voice.

"And to top it all off, they were a couple of my best customers but I cut them off. I wasn't going to have her swinging by to pick up their deliveries." Miles stood. "You said something about needing to use my computer?"

"Personal business only," he assured him. "I need to find out about a potential death."

The man vacated his seat, took his donut, and stood off to the side. He looked over Pain's shoulder as the big man sat and began to pound away. "I saw that your partner had been hit. Is it serious?"

"She'll live. If she doesn't, you will need a new business partner."

"In spite of what you may think of us, Jules is a very gifted doctor. He only went into the coroner side of medicine because he couldn't live with the guilt if one of his patients was to die under his care. Your partner is in good hands. It's my hands that are no longer as steady as they once were."

The ex-agent was beginning to think of the two as actual human beings, but now was not the time to delve into more of their histories. He was searching for the history of one Special Agent Marshal Buchanan.

A quick scan using the standard search engines came up with little of any use. A few press releases touted the man's successes as he rose through the FBI ranks, but little else.

"Make yourself useful, would you? Run to Iggy's room and tell Agony that I need her phone."

"And if she asks me why?"

"Tell her I want to order a pizza. And don't forget to say please."

Miles toddled off as quickly as he could, returned a few minutes later, and handed him the phone. "She said to hold the sausage. She's seen enough of them lately."

He laughed, scrolled through recently dialed numbers, and pressed one labeled, *HT*.

Pain had guessed right. The reporter answered on the first ring. *Does the man ever sleep?*

"Harry T, don't waste my time."

"Agony's in trouble and I need your help," he said bluntly

"Pain, first initial M. Talk to me. Is she hurt?" The reporter sounded concerned.

"Not mortally but she's pissed."

"That is never a good thing. What can I do?"

"Nothing for publication yet, okay? That's how you two work?"

"What...Do...You...Need? And please don't make me repeat the question. I was in the middle of a dream where I was about to be buried up to my neck in cabana girls and I'd like to get back to it as soon as possible." Harry made no effort to hide his impatience.

"You remember she mentioned a fed."

"Buchanan, yeah, yeah, clean as a whistle. No legs to that story."

"Maybe, maybe not," he conceded. "But I think he lost someone and is out for revenge. My problem is that I don't know who or when and I've done online searches for half an hour now."

"Hold on."

Holding on was not one of Pain's specialties but he didn't have much choice. Two minutes later, Harry T came back on the phone. "Are you at a computer?"

"That I am," he confirmed.

"Then type in this URL. That would be in the white bar at the top of the page."

"I know what a fucking URL is and where to put it," he protested.

"Why do you sound so pissed at me?" The reporter snorted. "You're the one who woke me up!"

"Sorry, Harry. What'd'ya got?"

Harry T read the URL. Pain typed it in and leaned back, open-mouthed.

"How did you do that?"

"I don't know," the other man answered. "But I suspect that a journalism degree from Northwestern followed by working for thirty years as an investigative journalist might have contributed a little to my know-how. Is that enough info for you to go on?"

"It's a damn good start. When the dust settles, you may end up with one hell of an exclusive."

"I'd better. Take good care of that girl, Pain, or I'll write your obituary myself and it won't be flattering."

Harry T ended the call and went back to try and recapture his cabana girls dream.

Pain turned to Miles. "I need this printed."

"What part?"

"All of it."

The man fumbled around to make sure there was enough paper in the printer and let the electronics do the rest. Five minutes later, Pain had the hard copies he needed and set off to check on his partner.

He found her seated upright on the table. She tried to flex her left arm and winced.

"He wants me to wear a sling!" she snapped indignantly.

"Only for a few days." The doctor defended himself hastily. "The bullet was a through and through and didn't fracture the bone, but a piece of it chipped off and lodged in a muscle. That is what caused the pain. Once I plucked the pesky piece out, all I had to do was add a few stitches and redo the bandages."

"And now he wants to confine me to a sling!" Agony repeated her complaint.

"Not her whole body. Only her arm and only for a few days."

"Will not wearing a sling make the injury worse?" Pain asked.

"It won't do the stitches any good if she decides to enter a tennis match."

"Got it. No tennis. I'll take her and the sling and we'll both let you get ready for your rush hour."

He helped her off the table and insisted that she wear the sling for at least a few hours. She griped but played the good patient, at least for the time being. They reached the entrance and neither Miles nor Ignatius stood at the door to wave goodbye, which was fine. Pain had snuck a screwdriver out and after swapping the Lexus' license plate for one from a hearse, they left.

"Where are we going?" she asked grumpily.

He didn't need a GPS to find the destination he had in mind. "The first stop is a no-tell. We need to get cleaned up, put our plans in order, and go out in the morning to get fresh clothes."

"On whose tab?"

"Miles assured me that this still has a grand on it," he said and pulled a credit card out. "He volunteered it so I wouldn't raid his inventory and in return, he promised to not report it stolen for forty-eight hours."

Twenty minutes later, he returned to the Lexus with the key to a double room at the Cavalier Motel. It was nothing fancy but no questions were asked when a still soot-covered Pain woke the night clerk and secured a room. Miles and Ignatius had both offered Agony some serious-strength pain meds, but she had declined. The Motrin would suffice and not leave her head all fuzzy in the morning.

He opened the door and led her inside. "I don't know about you but I need some sleep. I'll take the bed closest to the door. Let me know if you need me to sing you a lullaby. We have some serious shit to talk about when the morning comes."

Without any further comments, he stripped his smoke-scented shirt off and slid into his bed. She wanted to stay up, talk it all out, and make plans, but her arm ached and she could use a rest from the pain. She popped a couple of Motrin and slid into her bed. It only took rolling in the wrong direction once before her left arm reminded her that she might want to sleep on her right side that night.

The morning came much too early for either of them, but Agony was the second one to wake when Pain came in carrying a fast-food version of breakfast and two tall cups of coffee. He had also showered and wore a t-shirt that barely fit him and read, *Oh shit, you're not going to want to talk to me, are you?*

"Pickings were slim at the truck stop," he said by way of explanation.

He set the food down on the small desk and pulled out the copies of the web pages he had printed in Miles' office.

"Food for the body. Reading for the brain."

He took a biscuit and some hash browns from the bag, sat on his bed, and left the desk for her to use.

It wasn't easy to eat and read at the same time with the use of only one arm, but she managed. A short while later, she reached the same conclusion he had.

"Virginia Ruell."

"Ginny to her friends." Pain nodded.

Agony read out loud from the obituary. "Survived by… mother, father, two brothers, and one fiancé, Marshal Buchanan."

"Keep going. It gets worse."

She flipped through the pages. "A one-car accident in broad daylight. She drove over a guard rail and off a cliff."

A nibble here, a sip of coffee there, and a few more page flips turned up a whole new article about how the FBI had run into a stone wall regarding what had been labeled as The Gang of Five Investigation.

Special Agent Marshal Buchanan was quoted as saying that the investigation was still ongoing but no significant progress had been made. Although the FBI would make every effort to continue, until more verifiable leads were found, the agency would make no further announcements.

"Buchanan was the lead investigator on whatever this Gang of Five was?"

Pain nodded.

"And his fiancé died in the middle of it?"

He nodded again. "That's how I read it too. I'm not a big believer in coincidences when investigations are underway and someone dies. I don't know if it was a warning to Buchanan that he would be next or if it was simply to distract him."

She flipped another page and read out loud again. "Chief of Police, Chauncey Morris, announced that no foul play was found in the wreckage of Virginia Ruell's unfortunate accident." She looked up. "They stonewalled him."

"They stonewalled you when you were looking into All-in-Alex's death. SISTER stonewalled me when I tried to look into Kip's. We may have more in common with Special Agent Buchanan than we thought."

"True, but we can't go killing everyone involved, as tempting though it may be. Identifying them and bringing them to some type of court-backed justice or accountability, yes. But killing? In cold-blooded execution style? Not unless it came to a situation where it was either them or me."

"I don't think you and Buchanan are on the same page. He sent us to the lodge not to gather information that would hold up in court but to narrow the field of who he should focus on."

Agony was tired of beating herself up for having been taken in and used by Buchanan. "And we narrowed it down to Chauncey Morris. We may as well have painted a target on his head."

"I also think it helps to explain why he went after Ahjoomenoni so hard," Pain told her. "He knew he couldn't get to whoever murdered his fiancé through official channels, so he appeared to put all his energy into her, mostly for show. At the same time, he ran his black-ops to investigate and assassinate one or more high profile people, all of whom must have had a connection to the Moorfin."

"Ahjoomenoni became what you would call a dragon?" She could see the logic in it.

"Exactly. Look at me. Look who I'm going after. Look how hard I'm trying to move on from my fiancé and her unfortunate accident."

She was not proud of the next words she spoke. "We could always stand back and let him have his vengeance. I wouldn't approve of it but I could chalk it up as a sin of omission on our part for not stepping in."

"A sin that we may very well end up paying for." Agony gave him a questioning look. "Who has recently visited the Moorfin Lodge? Who has been seen arguing with Chief Morris? Remember, the lodge has video cameras everywhere—cameras that we unwittingly acknowledged and allowed when we checked in. Maybe they'll let our adventures there slide because the publicity could get extremely ugly. But if Morris is gunned down, the videos could be edited to make us prime suspects numbers one and two."

"Son of a bitch." She knew he was right.

"And not only Chief Morris but any other future deaths of lodge members. It could become a long list."

"And Buchanan's hands would be clean because his only focus has been on Ahjoomenoni." She scowled as she accepted the unpleasant ramifications.

The coffee had been acceptable and the breakfast almost edible, but the conversation and their conclusions left a less than pleasant taste in their mouths.

"How's the arm?" Pain asked after a few moments of silence.

Agony flexed a little and winced. "Better. More sore than painful. I think I can live without the sling."

"Thoughts?"

"Chief Morris will want to have us arrested or possibly shot on sight." She almost regretted not shooting him when she had the chance.

He sighed. "And he is the one person we need to protect and save."

"Where do we start?"

"We get to Bertha and use Miles' card for a nicer hotel room for tonight," he stated practically. "Then we'll see what we can come up with, hopefully before Buchanan makes his move."

CHAPTER SEVENTEEN

They could have afforded a hotel room on their own but neither wanted to dip into their emergency fund unless they had no choice. Besides, using Miles' card gave them the benefit of keeping their whereabouts unknown, at least for another day until he reported it as stolen. Their targets were Buchanan and Morris, and they were fairly certain that the same two would target them.

After retrieving Bertha, they wiped their fingerprints from the Lexus and left it parked in the most likely neighborhood to have it stripped and sold for parts. Pain carried the two suitcases and Agony, being the more presentable of the two, checked them into a two-bedroom suite in a modestly priced chain hotel.

Once in their suite, they both took long-overdue showers and met at the small dining room table where they pulled their laptops out.

"How often can we use your pal Harry T?" he asked.

"We've already stretched it with the info on Buchanan's fiancé. He will expect something in return and I'm not sure we'll have anything we can give him."

"Crap. Where do we even start? Do you know any psychics who can predict the chief's whereabouts in advance?"

"Sadly, no—but maybe I know the next best thing."

She pressed a few keys and quickly found what she was looking for. "Grab a pen and pad from the desk."

He did as instructed and sat again, ready to take notes. After a pause to gather her thoughts, she dialed and put the phone on speaker.

A friendly female voice answered on the third ring. "Department of Public Affairs, Officer Hanratty speaking."

"Yes, Officer Hanratty. This is Nichole Simons from the Star Tribune."

"What can I do for you, Ms. Simons?"

"I'm a reporter in the Lifestyle Section, and I'm calling to follow up on a conversation I had with Chief Chauncey Morris the other day."

"I wasn't aware that the chief had talked to any reporters." A slight skepticism crept into Officer Hanratty's voice.

"Oh, it wasn't an interview—no, no. I happened to run into him at the Moorfin Lodge and he seemed much more relaxed than he does at his usual buttoned-down public appearances. In fact, I was rather surprised. He was jovial, engaging, and had a sense of humor that I was not expecting. He even insisted that I call him Chance, not Chief Morris."

Pain smiled. So far, other than her name and occupation, his partner had spoken nothing but the truth.

"My, you must have made quite the impression."

"I don't know..." Agony's voice dripped modesty as she answered. "We were all out at the pool enjoying the afternoon and the last thing I wanted to do was to turn it into an interview. After all, one doesn't go to the Moorfin to work. But I did mention that he could be quite charming when his guard was down and asked if he would perhaps consider being featured in one of the Lifestyle's *Getting to Know You* segments. It's always one of our most popular articles."

"Oh, I love those! Are you the one who did the piece on the mayor?"

She sighed. "I wish. We're always in friendly competition and she's gloated about it ever since. Chance—I mean, Chief Morris—mentioned that he would attend a rather large public function in a few days and maybe I could start by catching up with him there. But as I said, we were at the poolside so I didn't have anything to write the details on and I'm afraid I forgot which function it was. I hoped you could maybe help to refresh my memory."

"Let me see." A pause followed while Officer Hanratty checked the schedule. "He was probably referring to the Condor Dinner."

"That's it! I remembered it was named after a bird but couldn't remember which one."

"It's scheduled for tonight and should be quite an affair," the woman told her. "According to the itinerary we've been provided, dignitaries from every country in South America will be there. The Andean Condor is the largest bird in the western hemisphere and is very endangered. The whole affair is a benefit to help raise money and awareness. Dinner, raffles, music, the whole shebang. But don't forget your press pass. The security will be very tight."

"Thank you, Officer Hanratty. You've been most helpful. Hopefully, the chief will remember me and spare me a few minutes."

Agony hung up before the officer could ask her to repeat her name or if she had any messages to pass on in case she ran into the chief.

"Bite me, Harry T!" She was rightfully proud of herself.

"I'm impressed." Pain was proud of her too. He had pounded the keys once the name Condor had been mentioned. "What I see here is that many upper-echelon international representatives will be there. Do you think Morris has enough influence to be an invited guest? This seems a little above his league."

"Maybe he's using some Moorfin connection," she suggested. "Another possibility is that there is bound to be a strong police presence there and maybe he will slip in as part of his duties to make sure everyone knows that under his command, the city can handle major events. Damn, I wish I had pressed harder on what the chief's role was."

"Don't sweat it. You did great. Either way, we now know where he will be tonight. And if we know it, the chances are that Buchanan does too. An event this large may make it easier for him to maneuver the chief into an unfortunate situation."

"Where is it being held?" Her mind had already turned to practical issues.

"The grand ballroom of the Guildmoor Hotel."

Agony uttered a low whistle. "I don't think they'll let us waltz in through the front door."

"I'm not sure we could even get in through the servant's entrance," he agreed. "How's your arm?"

"Will you stop asking me about my arm?"

"Sure, as soon as you stop wincing every time you move it."

"So what do we do? Break in through a basement window? Pretend we're health inspectors there to inspect the kitchen?"

Pain stopped his scrolling and looked up with a smile. "Remember how I said I don't believe in coincidences?"

"I've heard you say it a time or three, yeah."

"Well, I may have to start reassessing that."

"The reason being?" Her patience began to wear a little thin.

"The band is Vector Cinco. Have you ever heard of them?"

"Latin pop-rock or something, right? They had a few dance hits a decade or so ago."

"That's them," he confirmed. "They are out of Argentina,

which makes them perfect for a save the Andean Condor Campaign. I didn't realize they were performing again."

"So they got the band back together. Good for them." She couldn't help a little snark. "How does that affect us?"

"The lead singer, Juan Juarez, owes me a favor." He looked smug.

"How big a favor?"

Pain closed the laptop. "I saved his daughter's life."

Agony leaned back in her chair. "Now that's what I call a sizable favor."

"We have to change and get a move on." Before she could ask, he held a hand up. "I'll explain on the way."

"What do I change into?"

"Jeans, boots, work-type clothes. We'll be roadies for the night."

"A one-armed female roadie?" She snorted with dry amusement. "Oh yeah, I'll pass inspection."

"Fine, you can be a groupie. Do you still have the blonde wig? JJ always did have a weakness for blondes."

"I think I'll stick to being a roadie."

An hour later, the partners had checked out of the hotel and Pain was behind Bertha's wheel while Agony rested her arm.

"Juan did his best to keep it quiet and even changed his last name to Juarez when he got into music as a teenager. He wanted to make sure he made it on his own and not because of his family's influence."

"His family was influential?" For some reason, that surprised her.

"Only in the way that the vice president of a country would be." He let that sink in before he continued. "Juan paid his dues for over a decade and made it all on his own. The band had several songs climbing the charts and was in the middle of a very successful tour of the US when it was suddenly canceled with no explanation other than *Internal Band Strife* headlines. They returned home and disappeared from the public eye."

"Drugs?"

He shook his head. "Kidnapping."

"Oh."

"Kip and I were in Chile on another op when we were redirected to Argentina. A small, relatively insignificant gang of insurgents wanted to make some demands on the government. Their only problem was that they had very little name recognition, public support, or bargaining power. What they did have, though, was the knowledge that Juan Juarez's daughter was the grandchild of the vice president."

"Kidnappers one, vice president, zero?" The partners had worked a couple of kidnapping cases together and Agony knew how the deal would have played out.

"Which is where Kip and I came in. The US and Argentinian governments were involved in a few negotiations of their own at the time, and no one wanted the insurgents to distract from those. They also didn't want them to get any publicity with their demands. Juanita is probably around eighteen by now and the rebels were never heard from again."

"And Juan Juarez and Vector Cinco are the featured band tonight at the Condor Dinner."

"That about sums it up." He nodded. "All we have to do is find his tour bus, which will be parked nearby, and call in a favor."

"It beats the hell out of my plan," she confessed.

"Which was?"

"Which was to have you run interference while I ran into the ballroom screaming, 'Chauncey Morris is a pervert!'"

"Yeah." He grimaced. "How about we not go with that one?"

"Killjoy."

Special Agent Marshal Buchanan had already spent the previous night at the hotel. He'd had several options for gaining access to the Guildmoor, but using his FBI credentials to lie his way in was not one of them. Too many phone calls would have been involved as the security forces would try to verify the threat he claimed might be present, and none of the calls was likely to work to his benefit.

The advantage he had over Pain and Agony was that he had known Morris's probable attendance in advance of the dinner. Using a fake but valid credit card, he had simply booked himself a room the day before the event and went to work. He also had several other fake IDs handy—health inspector, homeland security officer, and INS agent. The last one could be extremely useful if he had to harangue one of the custodial staff or kitchen help for information or access to a specific room or closet.

He had the blueprints for the hotel already printed so he spent most of the afternoon in his room familiarizing himself with every nook and cranny of the hotel. If he had been there on official fed business, he could have used the afternoon to wander around, inspect rooms and hallways, and get a hands-on acquaintance with the building. That not being the case and with security cameras everywhere, even in the stairwells, he had to settle for the blueprints.

By ten o'clock the night before the dinner, he had decided that he needed to get a closer look at one particular area in person. Having little other recourse, he chose to visit the hotel bar and get seriously drunk.

There was a good-sized crowd at the tables, fairly raucous for the stately Guildmoor, but he managed to secure a stool near the end of the bar and soon realized the reason for the crowd and the noise. The South Americans were in town and the bar's television sets were all tuned to ESPN Deportes, where the Bolivian National Team was taking on Equador in a Friendlies match.

Not only did Buchanan think that soccer was one of the most boring sports to watch this side of cross-country skiing but he also had trouble with how passionate the fans could be. No matter how many bad calls an NFL referee might make during a game, no one ever waited hours in the parking lot after the games to accost them—often fatally.

But the boisterous crowd gave the agent all the distraction he needed to order a tall glass of water, which he drank quickly, and several vodka shots in quick succession. He poured these into his empty water glass. The shots kept coming, and the water level in his glass rose steadily.

Shortly before midnight, he ordered his last shot, paid his rather substantial tab, and left a decent tip. He swished the vodka around in his mouth to make sure that his breath would match his behavior and allowed himself to swallow. *Yes, sir.* He savored the taste and decided that he had received his money's worth. He would have to remember the brand the next time he ordered a martini.

"Morrison? Motley?" The earbuds crackled to life with the voice of Cleveland Jones, the overnight Security Supervisor.

"Yes, sir?" The answers came in simultaneously.

"We seem to have a guest on level three who is having difficulty finding his room."

"Danger assessment?" Motley asked.

"Only to his brain. He knocked back eight shots in an hour and a half."

It was Morrison's turn. "One of our international visitors?"

"Not with skin that pale. Get him out of my hallway and back into his room."

"Yes, sir," they responded simultaneously.

Buchanan stood in front of a door and fumbled with his room's keycard, even though the door had a standard lock. He saw the two security guards approaching from opposite ends of the hallway and slurred, "I can't find the shlott."

"That's because that is a keyed room, sir," Morrison, the larger of the guards informed him gently. "It is a maintenance room, not a guest room."

The agent held his card up and inspected it closely. "Oh, tha' s'plain's a lot." He fumbled in his pockets and pulled his car keys out. "I mus' need one o' these."

"No sir," the shorter, wiry guard explained. "Those are your car keys."

He stumbled back against the door. "I guesh no one wan's me to drive off with the hotel, huh?"

Buchanan laughed and stumbled forward into the big guard's arms.

"No sir," the man answered as the smaller guard relieved the drunk of his room's keycard. "No one wants that."

"Room three-forty-five," Motley said as he checked the number with his portable scanner.

"Well, at least he's on the right floor."

The two guards were able to escort the eight-shot guest to his room. They were even thoughtful enough to guide him to his bed, where he collapsed in a stupor. It would be very bad publicity to have a guest stumble and crack his skull open on the corner of an end-table and bleed to death on the floor.

"Have a good night, sir." Morrison backed slowly out of the bedroom.

"Wha'? No lullaby?"

"That's above our pay grade, sir." Motley followed his fellow guard out of the room and into the hallway and closed the door gently.

Morrison reported to their supervisor. "Guest safely escorted to bed, sir."

"Good job, guys. Can you two head to the pool? A few of our guests have decided that it is clothing optional."

"We're on our way," Motley confirmed and again wondered why the hotel had the policy of keeping the pool open twenty-four-seven.

Left alone, Buchanan sat, stashed the ring of keys he had lifted from the big guard's belt in his nightstand, and headed to his room's mini-bar for a seltzer. There would be a seven am shift change, which would be the time for him to visit the maintenance room and see what he could set up to welcome Police Chief Chauncey Morris the next evening.

By the time the next evening rolled around, Pain had caught up with Juan Juarez. The Vector Cinco tour bus was not hard to find since the side of it was painted to match the Argentinian flag with its alternating blue-white-blue stripes and a smiling sun in the center of the white.

Unlike when Vector Cinco had toured ten years earlier at the height of their fame, the bus didn't need a dozen security guards to surround it. This tour wasn't a comeback, per se, or an attempt to relive past glories. It was almost as if they tried to fly under the radar as they eased slowly into the public eye again.

Having found a safe place to park Bertha, Pain led Agony on the short walk as he approached the one roadie who stood as security outside of the bus.

"Could you please tell Mr. Juarez that Matias Payne is here to say hello?"

"Who the hell is Matias Payne?"

He didn't pull any macho attitude in response to the less than polite question. "That would be me. I am an old friend of Juan and his daughter Juanita. If he is available, I would like to say hello. If he is not available—because I know he must be busy—we will move on and enjoy the concert. It has been a long time. All I'm asking is for you to let my old friend, J-a-J know that Matias Payne is here to pay his respects."

The muscle-bound roadie knew two things for certain. One was that his boss had made it clear that JJ was a moniker that fanboys and girls used and he had never cared for it. The other thing was that Juan Juarez trusted him to sort the good from the time-wasters.

Pasqual the roadie held up a "give me a moment" finger and stepped to the side and out of hearing as he spoke into his mic.

A minute later, Juan Juarez stepped out of the bus, took one look at his visitor, and sang, "Matias, Matias, where have you got e-us?"

The two men embraced. Pain turned to Agony and introduced her. "This is Ms. Alicia Goni. Her friends simply call her Agony."

Juan took her hand and kissed it. "And what do your enemies call you?"

"Much the same thing," the ex-agent answered for his suddenly silent partner

J-a-J took a step back and spoke with that damned Latin-lover accent that Pain could never hope to pull off. "Ahh, Miss Agonìa. Sometimes, we must suffer before we find beauty. But in your case, perhaps it is in reverse?"

For the first time since Pain had met her, she was speechless.

"I need a favor, Juan."

The tone in Matias The Gift of God Payne's voice brought the other man up short.

"A favor such as the one you once performed for my father and myself?"

"Similar, yes."

"Then ask, my friend. I will deny you nothing."

"We need passes that will give us backstage access."

"Pasqual! Two passes for my friends, por favor!"

"On it!"

The roadie hustled into the bus and came out with two laminated passes that he looped over their necks.

Juan Juarez kissed Pain full on the lips. "That kiss was meant for Miss Agonìa. Please pass it along for me. And the next time you need a favor from me, make it one more difficult to provide. Otherwise, I shall put you on my list of boring people I wish to avoid."

With that and a smile, Juan Juarez climbed into his bus and waited for the call to come inside for the sound-check. This would be one of the major events in the resurgence of Vector Cinco.

Not only would tonight's concert be for a good cause, but he would also be able to perform knowing that he had repaid a small portion of the debt he owed to the man who had saved his daughter's life. *Oh, yes,* he vowed. *Tonight, everyone will dance!*

Everyone did end up dancing but not to the same drummer.

Chauncey Morris, dressed in his finest blue uniform complete with every medal he had earned while working his way to the top, did his dance as an uninvited peacock. The police chief preened while he inspected his troops where they stood guard around the dignitaries assembled in the ballroom as dinner was finishing and tables were being cleared to make room for the musical portion of the evening. He had failed to finagle an invitation to the dinner but after moving around the crowd, he decided it was just as well.

Why can't these fucking people speak English? If he had been seated at a table during the dinner and speeches, all he would have been able to do would be to nod and chuckle when everyone else did because he wouldn't have understood a damn word his tablemates had said. With that revelation, he decided that maintaining an impressive posture from a distance was his best move.

He circled the main room, did some glad-handing with a handful of local politicians and judges, several of them lodge members, but mostly remained on the periphery to keep his presence noticeable but not intrusive.

Buchanan's dance would be done in the maintenance room on the third floor. All he had to do was lure Chauncey Morris away from his boys in blue sycophant brigade, which wouldn't be hard to do with the plan he had in mind.

Pain and Agony's dance was to avoid the main ballroom where the dinner, followed by a handful of speeches and Vector Cinco's performance, would be held and keep an eye out for a police chief and a rogue fed while trying to remain in the shadows.

Chauncey Morris, the strutting peacock, was easy for the partners to locate. Buchanan, not so much. It wasn't until one of Chief Morris's boys whispered into his ear and handed him an envelope that the partners' antennas went up.

Morris opened the envelope, glanced inside, and smiled. He motioned for several of his men to follow him as he headed to the elevators.

Pain was suddenly pissed. "Shit! How high is he going?"

Agony led the way hastily out of the shadows where they'd been watching and into the middle of the hotel lobby, flashing her backstage pass at any and all security details. "I'm with the band!"

She leaned closer to Pain as they watched the elevator Chauncey Morris had entered. "Damn, I've always wanted to say that."

The lights paused on the third floor and descended to the

lobby, where the elevator doors opened to show the car was empty.

"I guess the third floor it is." Pain led the way to the stairwell.

Behind him, Agony proudly announced at least twice to whoever had asked, "I'm with the band."

They reached the right level and he took a quick peek into the hallway before he motioned for her to follow. That wing was empty, so they walked past the elevators and turned the corner as innocently as a couple of guests returning to their rooms. A third of the way down, they passed four boys in blue standing guard outside a room with a *Private Party* sign placed over where the room number would normally be.

"Some kind of private party must be going on, huh?" He laughed as he passed the guards.

There was no humor in the reply. "Very private."

The partners continued to their non-existent room. Agony chose one at random, began to fumble through her purse, and spoke loudly enough for the guards to hear. "I thought you were the one in charge of the room key tonight."

"Well, *darling*, you thought wrong. It's got to be in there somewhere. Let me look."

"Trouble in paradise." One of the cops snickered and garnered a chuckle from the other three.

"That room didn't have a number," Pain mumbled as he fumbled through her purse.

Agony raised her voice as she snatched her purse back. "Do you think I didn't know that? What are you going to do now? Pick the lock?"

"I bet you I could do it!"

The cops watched the woman shake her head at her idiot partner. "Don't you think it would be easier to simply ask for assistance or are you too macho for that?"

Agony left the squabble and hurried toward the officers, her man trailing behind. She had a nice smile, and four of the cops asked the eternal question most men did when they saw a mismatched couple—*What is she doing with a buffoon like that?*

"Could one of you kind gentlemen please assist us in getting into our room?"

"Sorry, ma'am. As much as we'd like to, we are police officers, not bellhops. You will have to return to the front desk for assistance."

She stormed between the four and split the brigade in half. Pain disabled the two on the left with a kidney punch and a chop to an ear and as the two remaining officers looked at their fallen comrades, she felled them both with a couple of non-lethal but morning-headache-inducing baton strikes to the back of their heads.

Knowing that the hallways were monitored and with four disabled cops now on the floor, Pain didn't take the time to try to pick the lock. Instead, he delivered one swift heel-first kick to break the handled side of the door in but leave the hinges still intact. He flung all four bodies into the room ahead of them and marched in and over them.

Agony followed quickly and closed the door behind her. She couldn't secure it enough to stop anyone else from entering, but the whole episode in the hallway had taken less than six seconds. The odds were on their side that anyone in the hotel's main security room had not had their eyes directed at a third-floor hallway, especially when there were so many other activities to keep track of.

They didn't know what to expect when they'd busted through the door of the room, but a row of ceiling-to-floor plush velvet curtains would not have been high on either of their lists.

CHAPTER EIGHTEEN

"Are we about to enter a porn shoot?" Pain sounded suitably horrified.

"With Chauncey Morris involved, anything is possible."

A familiar special agent's voice called, "There's no need to knock. The curtains aren't locked."

Pain slipped a gun out of the holster of one of Morris's unconscious officers, gave it to his partner to use instead of one of her own if necessary, and motioned for her to take her baton and the gun to the left-hand side of the curtain. Once she was in position, he separated the two curtains and walked through the middle.

There was a fair amount to take in, but Special Agent Marshal Buchanan didn't seem to pose any immediate threat. He had a gun but he had it trained on Police Chief Chauncey Morris, who no longer wore his dress blues with all the medals and looked like he wished he had skipped the whole fancy dinner affair.

"I don't know which end of the curtains you chose, Agony," Marshal called, "but I assure you that it's safe for you to come out. You are not on my list yet."

She kept the borrowed cop's gun raised and entered. Two stunning, provocatively-dressed women sat quite comfortably off to the side on a makeshift sofa of tarps and cushions, one blonde, one brunette, and both of them coked out of their heads.

The agent shrugged as he explained at least part of the scene. "They are a couple of high-priced escorts who owed me a favor. A hand-delivered envelope that included a photo with a handwritten invitation and two fresh lipstick-kisses was all it took to lure the chief here for a private party."

Marshal looked at the partners and out of professional courtesy and curiosity asked, "What ruse did you use?"

Agony held her pass up and smiled as she wondered how much more mileage she could get out of the line. "I'm with the band."

Pain held his pass up too. "Good roadies are hard to find."

"Creative. I'm impressed." The agent raised an eyebrow.

"Your ruse?" he asked Marshal.

"I paid for a room yesterday, got stinking drunk at the hotel bar last night, and lifted the keys off one of the night security guards who had to help me to my room. I've been in here ever since the seven o'clock shift change this morning. This is more of a boiler room than a maintenance closet, so unless the HVAC blows or the water suddenly shuts off, no one comes in here very often. I've had all day to set it up as my private playground. I did, of course, jimmy the lock but so far, I've had no visitors until the gold-dust twins opened the door to welcome the guest of honor."

Honor was not the word that sprang to either of the partner's minds when they finally took in the whole scene.

Pain didn't know where to begin so he started with simple logistics. "We weren't more than five minutes behind. How, in those five minutes, did you manage to get Chief Morris into that outfit?"

Buchanan sighed. "It's not the outfit I wanted but all the Frank-N-Furter costumes were out of stock and I had to go with

Little Bo Peep, so that cut down some of the time. The girls didn't need any time at all to convince the chief to drop his clothes voluntarily. Once I made a sudden appearance with my little influencer"—Buchanan held his Magnum up —"he became very adept at being a quick-change artist."

"What stopped him from calling for his backup and hoping they could bust the door down in time?"

"He knew me and knew that since he helped to murder my fiancé—I assume you've learned about that by now?"

Both partners nodded, and Agony picked up their part of the conversation with sincere condolences. "I'm sorry for your loss, *Special* Agent Buchanan."

"Fuck the title. Ginny was the only thing that ever made me feel special. Morris knew that I had little left to live for, so if he cried out for help, the first shot fired would have gone straight into his head and other good officers' lives would have been lost. He knew my life wasn't something I was worried about as long as I could avenge Ginny's murder before I joined her."

Chief Morris might have added to the conversation but had been silenced very efficiently. He stood on a chair in his Little Bo Peep finest with his hands tied behind his back. A silken noose around his neck had been looped on an overhead pipe and he had another piece of silk bunched in his mouth to prevent him from crying out. His only contribution was to shoot bolts of panic and threats from his eyes. The eye-bolts proved extremely easy to avoid.

Agony kept her focus on the agent who, in spite of how deliberately he had set them up, she still held out some hope for.

"This isn't the way it has to end, Marshal."

"Ooh, we're resorting to Hostage Negotiations 101 now, are we? Let's use first names, shall we? We're merely friends sitting around chatting here, right?"

Buchanan walked calmly past them and through the velvet curtains. He held a taser up for them both to see in case they worried about his intentions. Four quick zaps ensured that none of Morris's four blue-uniformed guards would disturb them for at least another half-hour.

He stepped through the curtains again, still holding his Magnum, but didn't aim it in either of the partners' direction. "Relax, you two are not on my enemies list. If we had met under different circumstances, the three of us might have had a chance to become best of friends. I have no desire to be the agent of your demises."

She didn't completely buy it. "Our recent adventures at the Moorfin Lodge seem to belie that fact."

Pain was still on high alert as he wandered off to inspect the rest of the large boiler room, looking for any secret exits or other traps as he let Agony continue with her negotiator role with a fed who might have gone around one bend too many.

Buchanan apologized. "I wish I could offer you both chairs while I explained that, but I'm afraid I wasn't expecting company. Oh, and don't worry!" he called to Pain. "There are no exits or cameras. You would think a room this important to the entire building's infrastructure might have something a little more sophisticated than a handful of sprinklers, an alarm panel or two, and a couple of pull in case of emergency boxes. Seriously, the architect should be fired!"

The agent wandered to the chair the chief was standing on and lifted his Bo Peep skirt to peek under it. He let the skirt drop and took a step back.

"Oh, dear, Miss Peep. I don't think you will be able to hook any sheep around the neck to help guide them home with such a tiny little staff."

Morris wanted to kick out at the pissant agent but was terrified of losing his balance. Having a noose around one's neck while standing on a chair could do that to a person.

Buchanan took a stance behind the chair, ready to yank it out at any moment, and made what he thought was a perfectly polite and reasonable request.

"Could the three of us please have a civilized conversation? Because I do owe both of you an explanation."

Pain had finished his inspection of the room and returned to his partner's side hauling two three-foot stepladders he had found stacked in a far corner. There had also been four twelve-foot step ladders for the maintenance workers to use while repairing the higher pipes crisscrossing the ceiling, but for the immediate purposes, the short ones seemed to be of the most optimal use.

The agent smiled. "I must have missed those. So good, we are all comfy now. First, I would like to apologize."

"Apologize for past or future mistakes?" Agony returned to her negotiator's role.

"For the past, of course, at least regarding you two. Future mistakes have yet to be made."

"So says the Zen-master of mistakes," Pain muttered, which earned him a keep your mouth shut look from his partner as they sat on the short ladders.

"We're listening."

This was her first attempt to be a semi-official negotiator, but one thing she had learned while on the force and listening to the trained negotiators do their jobs was that keeping the subject talking seemed to be rule number one.

Buchanan began to slowly circle the chair where the chief balanced in his Bo Peep outfit. Morris' eyes now closed as if he feared he might die from humiliation as his three main enemies bandied words with each other.

"I will admit that I did not have an exit strategy set up for you two when I sent you to the Moorfin."

Her voice changed from one of calm to one of ice. "We eventually realized that on our own."

"Knowing your history, I had all trust in the world that you two would manage to make your escape."

"And if not, your hands would have remained clean. What are a couple of PI's to a fed when everyone knows he has focused all his attention on bringing Ahjoomenoni down?"

The agent had grace enough to nod at Agony's point. "I know. That was my bad. And yet here you both are, confirming my faith in your abilities to survive."

"Why us?" Pain interjected. "And why now?"

"Why you? Because I had you leveraged with Ahjoomenoni. Why now? Because whoever was responsible for Ginny's death knew I would never let it go, no matter how much it seemed like I had. Someone had to know I was coming for them. I had heard some chatter through various channels and knew I only had a matter of days left to track those responsible and confirm my suspicions before they came after me."

Buchanan moved behind the chair Morris stood on and poked him with the muzzle of his Magnum. He kept it outside the dress but aimed directly at where the chief's asshole would be.

"What do you think, Chiefy Peepy? Should I simply put a round up your ass and scramble your brains right now?"

In response to the suggestion, Chief Morris shook his head as a definitive no.

"Thanks to you two, I learned that Graybeard, Heironymous Rolf, Bolf, whatever, was merely a puppet. Chiefy-boy here was pulling the strings."

"But the Moorfin takes videos of everything. Even if they've edited them by now, surely enough guests have copies that we can trace. Every guest receives a video as a going-away present."

Buchanan appreciated Agony's suggestion but scoffed at the reality.

"Sure. How about we approach a judge and request warrants for all DVDs that the Moorfin's guests have been given at check-out for the last four days? I'm sure that will gain some serious traction. Most of the DVDs have already been altered to show the two of you and your confrontations with Chief Morris."

"The fucker tried to garrote me!" She hadn't managed to let that little detail slide into the recesses of her memory banks yet.

The agent had a hard time understanding why they hadn't caught on yet to what they and he were up against. "Proper police restraint procedure. The camera angles probably show Chief Morris trying to subdue a dangerous assailant who threatened one of the lodge's most distinguished members with nothing more than a basic police move to incapacitate an attacker from behind before she could do any more damage. On the edited video, it will probably show him from behind with his arms around your shoulders as he tried to get you gently onto the floor where you would be more manageable after the spur of the moment anger wore off."

"Shit." Pain hated it when the man was right. "He has a point."

Buchanan continued, still hoping that they would come around to his way of thinking. "I have many points. One is that none of any evidence you two obtained while at the Moorfin would stand up in a court of law. You were not officially there. There were no warrants and no lives in immediate danger, so you had no reason at all to be involved in what you observed or did. Any actions you took could be countermanded by dozens of witnesses who saw nothing but an out-of-control couple who were not enjoying their stay."

"We were never out of control!" Agony was firm.

"Even when Pain took a naked swan-dive from a third-floor balcony into the pool?"

"What?" The question exploded simultaneously from both partners.

"Think of me what you will. But I did have at least one person in place to try to help cover your backs the best he could."

The partners drew a deep breath. She exhaled hers first.

"Who?"

"A Moorfin hired hand. For the last two years, he worked the pool area, the grounds-keeping, and the stables. Wherever he was needed, Jimmy did his best to make himself one of the Moorfin's most valuable employees. He was also Ginny's younger brother."

The penny dropped and Agony picked it up.

"That is how you knew you were running out of time."

Buchanan nodded. "He is also why half the ATVs were not functional when you two made a run for it. He is one of the reasons you two are still alive today."

"And Jimmy?" she asked for both her and Pain.

"After two years of valuable service, Jimmy has been promoted to the Moorfin's Security Detail. He will remain my eyes and ears inside the lions' den."

"So why can't we use him for another year to gather what he can?"

The agent wanted to kick something and wondered why they seemed to have suddenly surrounded their brains with wisps and vapors. "Gather what, Ms. Goni? Overheard rumors? Plans of misdeeds that came to joyous fruition amongst the proud and the privileged? The Moorfin's roots run deep. Judges? DAs? Hell, for all I know, even the court stenographers could mistype a word or two in a trial's transcript if the price was right. Not to mention whatever blackmail could be going on behind the scenes."

He took a step back from the chair the chief was standing on.

"Marshal, don't!" Agony pleaded.

"Morris may not be the only snake but he is the one who bit me where it hurts. The same way he bit your partner, All-in-Alex, when you two came too close to stumbling onto the dirty work his cops were doing to help manipulate voting districts to benefit one of chiefy here's close Moorfin friends who was involved in a tight re-election campaign."

She was stunned. "How do you know that?"

"The same way I know that Pain, first initial M, when needing to use a public restroom, will always choose a stall in the farthest corner against a wall to sit in and take a piss. He would never allow someone to come in and attack him from behind while he had his zipper down and was focused on the urinal in front of him."

Agony looked at her partner, who nodded his affirmation.

"Alex was killed because of a voting issue?"

Buchanan thought he might have finally won her to his side. "That, and only that. Alex was a good cop and from what I have learned, a very loving father. The only reason he died was because the powers that be at the Moorfin decided that their lives would become much less complicated if there was one less honest cop in the world."

She turned to her partner again. "Pain?"

"I hate to say it but I believe he is speaking the truth, the whole truth, and nothing but the truth. But that doesn't mean he should be the judge, the jury, and the executioner."

For the first time, the agent aimed his Magnum at the partners, daring them to stop him as he smiled and kicked the chair out from under Chief Morris' feet.

The man's body dropped and Agony fired. Special Agent Marshal Buchanan never fired a shot of his own before his body hit the floor. Pain rushed to hold the chief up to prevent death from activities related to erotic asphyxiation.

"I need the chair!" he called.

Swallowing the vomit that threatened to rise from her stomach, she righted the chair and he guided the chief's feet onto it. That was all the courtesy they were willing to extend to Bo Peep at the moment.

The partners took a step back and looked at the body of Special Agent Marshal Buchanan. Her shot had hit his heart dead center and stopped all blood flow. He was finally at rest and his face looked almost peaceful.

Her voice, once she found the strength to speak, sounded

weak but firm. "I believe in my heart, Pain, that he was once a good man."

"Weren't we all." He sighed.

The partners shared a moment of silence to honor a man who had been pushed to a limit he had not been able to find his way back from.

CHAPTER NINETEEN

"Well, maybe not all." Pain amended his previous comment as they focused on the seemingly unrepentant and now thoroughly pissed-off-looking chief of police. He had regained his footing on the chair, a noose still around his neck and dressed as if he had lost his sheep and didn't know where to find them.

Pain made a simple request. "I'll need a hand."

"A hand for what?" Agony didn't sound antagonistic as much as curious.

Her partner lifted the body of Special Agent Marshal Buchanan and carried it into a darker part of the maintenance room that she hadn't had the time to explore.

"A hand to open the chute."

She trailed behind as he explained his intentions.

"Buchanan was too smart to leave any trace of him ever having been here. There is a chute up ahead I will need you to open. It leads directly to the hotel's furnace. The agent's body and bones will be incinerated. As far as anyone will know, he may have simply decided to retire and drop completely off the grid. For all his faults, he doesn't deserve to be involved in this."

"What about Ginny's brother Jimmy?"

"We'll find a way to let him know that his sister's death has been avenged. It is time for him to move on and build a life of his own. The past is now done with. The future still lies ahead."

They reached a dark-red two-by-two-foot door. Despite having only one good arm, she managed to open it and he slid the body gently into the chute before he closed the door.

Other than Chief Bo Peep Morris and the coked-out call girls, no one knew that Special Agent Marshal Buchanan had ever stepped foot inside the Guildmoor Hotel. The disappearance of an FBI agent was not something anyone in the bureau would take lightly but seven days later, a postcard from Fiji arrived at Buchanan's home office. The back of the postcard had a perfectly forged handwritten note that read, *Had enough. The weather is here, I wish you were beautiful.*

All the agents who had known him knew that he was a big Jimmy Buffett fan, so none of them questioned it. Agony didn't need to know how her partner had acquired a contact on Fiji who was also an excellent handwriting forger. But those questions only came up days later.

On this evening, in the maintenance room on the third floor of the Guildmoor Hotel, it was now time for the partners to clarify the details with the involved parties so that everyone would be able to keep their facts straight.

Chief Morris still stood on the chair in his Little Bo Peep finest and wished he could shout threats and curses. Unfortunately, he still had his hands tied behind his back and a small ball of satin stuffed in his mouth.

Pain had learned to offer suggestions as opposed to orders when it came to dealing with his partner, so he suggested, "How about I gather the girls and you take some pics?"

"That works for me." Her left arm still caused her pain, no matter how hard she tried to hide it, but taking a few photos with her phone while her partner did all the heavy lifting? That she could manage.

Chief Morris was easy for him to handle, what with him being all dressed and trussed up. The stoned out of their gourds call girls took a little more effort, but he managed. She moved around the room, careful to keep him out of the shots as he positioned and held the high-priced hookers up into as many compromising positions he could come up with while keeping their faces away from the view of her photos.

He only interrupted the process once and that was to give the chief's protective detail one more taste of the late, lamented Special Agent Marshal Buchanan's taser.

The photo-shoot done, the call girls lost themselves again to the pharmaceuticals that someone who said he was an FBI agent named…named…named…aw, who the hell cared? They had earned a grand each for a one-night gig and all the drugs they could ingest.

Pain and Agony scrolled through the photos she had recently taken while they left the chief still standing on his chair.

"Oh, I like this one." She handed her partner her phone. "How did you manage to hold them both up at the same time?"

"Neither one of them weighs more than one-twenty soaking wet. It wasn't too hard. And it's not like either of them wore suits of armor."

She had to agree with his last point. A sparrow could have easily carried off all the clothing the hookers had worn to line its nest without working up a sweat.

"Hey, Pain?"

"Yes?"

"Do birds ever sweat?"

That was a damn good question that he had never thought to ask himself. Before he and his partner had a chance to pursue the question further, their attention to the photos and the bird-sweating debate was disrupted by a ruckus being raised by the man on the chair.

Pain sighed. "Damn. Another country wants to chime in."

Agony moved toward the chair the ruckus-maker stood on and asked for her partner's advice.

"Shall I simply kick the chair out of the way and let gravity do its thing?"

"I am usually on the side of gravity," he told her and she readied her kick. "But in this case, I don't want to save the asshole's life twice in the same night."

"You are simply no fun anymore." She pulled the gag out of Morris's mouth and almost immediately regretted it as the chief launched into a verbal rampage.

"You are both under arrest for involvement in the kidnapping of the chief of police, the assault on four police officers, aiding and abetting prostitution, drug running, and the murder of a federal agent. Do you wish to cop a plea now or would you rather wait to consult your attorneys?"

Agony put her good hand on the back of the chair. "Would you mind if I borrowed this for a few minutes so I can sit and think it over?"

"You wouldn't dare."

"Oh, shit!" Pain scooped his partner up and carried her a short, safe distance away before he put her on her feet.

"What?" Agony protested loudly enough for the chief to hear her lie. "Do you think that with all the video and recordings we took while at the lodge of the chief and his sick coven of perverts, anyone will give his death from sexual activity gone bad a second thought?"

"Granted. And I'm sure others at the Moorfin will be ready to take over his role as headmaster." He looked at the chief's current outfit again. "Or headmistress, but I think he might be more useful to us alive than dead."

Morris snorted. "I won't be any use to you at all except as the one who is responsible for putting you both behind bars."

Pain approached the chief slowly. "Look. I'm trying to save

what's left of your miserable life here, so would you mind shutting the fuck up for a few minutes?"

The man couldn't seem to grasp his vulnerability. "No one is allowed to take videos while at the lodge. That is clearly stated in the welcoming package that you agreed to. Only lodge-approved videos are agreed to."

"Damn. I guess we didn't read the fine print."

Although he still stood on the chair, Morris was getting his bearings and felt more like his feet were on solid ground, at least legally speaking. "Well, you should have. Because if you had, you would realize that Buchanan was correct when he said that nothing you recorded would stand up in a court of law."

Agony strode forward, sore arm and all and with the memory of the chief trying to garrote her still fresh in her memory, and laughed.

"We're not concerned with having to prove anything in a court of law. In this instance, the court of public opinion would be much more powerful. Harry Tribelescheau is champing at the bit to run an exposè piece on you and your Moorfin connections."

At the name of Harry Tribelescheau, the chief lost much of his bluster. Harry T had been a pain in his ass for a long time, always looking for an angle to make him look bad. With the pictures they had taken combined with whatever action they had managed to capture while at the lodge, life as he knew it would be over.

She dug the knife in deeper and gave it an extra little twist. "How many of your Moorfin friends do you think will come out and publicly defend you? They will treat you as a leper. A one-off pervert who they had no idea was so twisted. We don't need to bring down the whole lodge. Harry can make it appear as if you were the only one there with such odd proclivities."

"She has a point, Chief. And knowing what I know of Harry T, I'm sure he can dig deeper and come up with a few less-than-legal activities you have been involved in that had nothing to do with the lodge."

Agony circled the chair and no longer felt the urgent need to yank it out.

"If I kick the chair, Chief, you will be left dangling from a pipe. If I give you to Harry T, you will be left dangling in the wind. So you see, unlike Special Agent Marshal Buchanan, I don't feel the need to be the one to kill you personally. Without your power and prestige, I assume there will be a long line waiting to assist you on your way to your well-earned eternal rewards."

Morris tried to regain some of his bluster. "Are you going to cut me down or kick the chair out? Because frankly, I am beginning to think I might die from boredom at any moment now."

"Well then." Agony laughed. "A happy ending all around. But here's the deal, Chief. My partner and I have never had a bitch before but I am warming up to the idea. We will wring you dry, every last drop, until you are no longer any use to us. Then we'll decide whether or not to hand everything we have to Harry T, at which point, it will be your choice whether to swallow a bullet from your gun or spend the rest of your life taking it up the ass from your new celly, Thunderdick. And until that time, you will call off any and all investigations you might have running into our suspected activities, will keep your manipulations to a minimum, and cancel the hit on me."

"I don't think you'll get a better offer, *Chance*. I've seen her in this kind of mood before. It never ends well for the other party. You might end up wishing we'd let Buchanan finish the job."

The chief took a few minutes to run the calculations. "You're saying you want me to mind my own business and you'll mind yours?"

She nodded. "And if you ever get a phone call from us, you will either answer it or return it immediately because it will be us calling in a favor for some information. I assure you that neither of us wants to talk to you any more than absolutely necessary, so the calls will not be an everyday occurrence but they will come."

"And the Moorfin?"

"What the fuck do we care about the Moorfin? Other than the fact that you waggled your dick in our faces, tried to garrote me, and then kill us both? Trust me, none of those facts will ever be forgotten. But we are people on a personal crusade like Buchanan. We would much prefer to try the live and let perverts live approach."

Pain appreciated the self-control his partner had shown when she'd reined herself in but didn't want the conversation to end quite yet. He guided her to the side and took her place circling the chief. This would be a tricky conversation to hold since he wanted to make sure he made solid eye contact with the man while also making sure that he could stop her from making any rash moves. If a stone could speak, the voice he now used would have matched it for the hardness it carried.

"What you and the Moorfin Gang did to his fiancé goes beyond the pale in my book. And we now know that you are also partly responsible for the hit put out on Alejandro Infante, a cop who was under your command. Of course, none of this can be proven. But once you are rescued, you will make it one of your top priorities to set up a Scholarship Fund in his name at Camden University."

"Camden?" This was the first Agony had heard about this plan.

"Camden specializes in the creative arts." He smiled. "Painting, sculpture, music, and woven-work skills, some of which may even involve knitting and weaving. Full tuition, room, and board. And you, Chief Chauncey Morris, shall take it upon yourself to convince your high-powered friends at the Moorfin to help keep the scholarship money flowing for one deserving young artist per year to be able to attend one of our state's best-kept secrets."

He turned to Agony. "No one attends Camden to come out

with a diploma that will put them on the fast track to becoming a lawyer. It is a gentle campus, set in the rolling upstate hills. Money and high GPAs don't matter. Pursuit of the creative arts is the name of the game there. Your approval is requested."

"My approval is granted."

Pain turned to the man of the hour again. "Chief?"

"Yeah, yeah. Full ride at Camden. Got it. Will you two get me down now?"

He hated to disappoint such a cooperative Bo Peep, but he shook his head. "No. Sorry. That is not in our job description. What we will do is leave as quietly and unobtrusively as possible. There are four of your boys in blue bodyguards who have been through one knock-out blow and two tasings each while trying to protect you."

"Three tasings." Agony held up a finger count in an effort at accuracy.

"Three?" He frowned in thought, then shrugged. "Either way, I think they deserve the honor of being able to claim that they rescued you."

"While I'm trussed and dressed like this?" Morris was once again seriously pissed off.

Pain made sure that the hookers were still breathing and took hold of Agony's good hand to lead her toward the velvet curtains. "Oh, I'm sure you can offer them some kind of incentives to keep the details to themselves. Promotions. Vacations. Transfers to another unit where they will never have to see you again."

She got her last dig in. "You can be quite creative when the need arises, Chief Bo Peep."

Once through the velvet curtains, the partners stepped carefully over the four boys who were once again beginning to come around.

Agony paused. "Do you still have the taser?"

"Well, duh." Pain held it up.

"I need it." She snatched it from his hand and applied another round to Morris's bodyguards. "There. I said it was three." She handed it to Pain. "We have to be able to give Harry T something."

They stepped out the door, walked calmly arm in arm down the hallway, turned the corner, and with perfect timing, caught the elevator on its downward path to the lobby.

The music and the beats from the grand ballroom echoed through the whole first floor. Juan Juarez and Vector Cinco were on fire and gave the guests their money's worth.

CHAPTER TWENTY

"I'm with the band!" Agony announced with a smile and flashed her backstage pass again as they hurried through the lobby, turned left on the sidewalk, and headed off as quickly as they could to retrieve Bertha.

She tucked the pass that had become one of her most cherished possessions in a pocket, pulled her phone out, and pressed redial.

"Harry T. Don't waste my time."

"Guildmoor hotel. Third-floor maintenance room. Chief of Police Chauncey Morris has been abducted, drugged, and held hostage. His personal security detail will rescue him in about twenty minutes. Don't waste any time getting there."

"Were you and your psycho partner involved?"

"I love you too, Harry!" Pain called, which earned him another elbow from his partner's good arm in his ribs.

"Only in a very peripheral kind of way, Harry," she assured him.

"Legs?"

"None that I can confirm. This is a one-off."

The call dropped.

In earlier days, Harry T would have been able to call, "Stop the presses!" as he chased a late-breaking story to beat the other daily papers to a morning edition headline. Having pissed off one too many editors, he now wrote for a weekly independent, in-depth paper. But he had also adapted to the times and with his reputation, had established a daily blog titled *Harry T and the Truth*.

He missed the days when everyone subscribed to the daily papers and would scan through them over their first cup of coffee. Some folks would turn to the funny pages first. Others would turn to the editorials. Some would turn to the obituaries and once they realized no one they knew was mentioned, would turn to the front pages to read through what had been happening.

Harry, with his blog, had gained a dedicated following. Some days, he would simply write *Nothing much going on* and leave it at that. He didn't want to waste anyone's time any more than he wanted anyone to waste his. But he had roused his photographer roommate Jose out of bed and together, they had reached the third floor of the Guildmoor in time to capture four policemen leading Chief Morris, wearing his dress blues as opposed to his white dress, out of the maintenance room.

Jose had snapped the photos as Harry got his money quote from Chief Morris. "I was abducted, drugged, and threatened in an effort to stop an ongoing investigation. But the law must prevail. These four officers caught wind of it and came to my rescue. The perpetrators escaped, but these brave officers saved my life. That is my only comment at this time."

The daily papers eventually picked up on the story, but all of the security footage from the cameras on the third floor of the Guildmoor had experienced a technical glitch during the chief's abduction, so Harry T and Jose had the exclusive all to themselves while the other reporters scrambled to catch up over the next several days.

He didn't pay the dailies any mind as they tried to come up with whatever they could piece together. Their reporters were not much more than cute little bear cubs and he was a full-grown grizzly. He knew Agony had lied when she'd said that the story didn't have any legs, but he also knew damn well that she knew he knew she was lying. That was how things worked with reliable sources.

Her partner—who frankly scared the hell out of him—had used her phone to call him for info on a dead girl, who ended up being the fiancé of an FBI agent who had been in the middle of a high-level investigation. He had sent Pain enough info to guide him and Agony in the right direction but had also done some digging on his own.

Agony had repaid that with her heads-up about the third floor of the Guidmoor so they were all square in the favor department.

When all recent calls were taken into consideration, along with what had—and more importantly, had not been said—Harry T knew that somewhere, something dark was going on in the shadows. He loved nothing more than shining a bright light into the murky corners to expose the creepy crawlies. Especially if he was the first one to pick up the scent.

After they had retrieved Bertha, the partners had dug into their own pockets and showing up at two in the morning, had managed to find an available two-bedroom suite at another chain hotel that served a continental breakfast starting at 6:00 am. Scrambled eggs, toast, a variety of pork offerings, freshly baked —*yeah, right*—muffins, and something resembling coffee was at least filling. The beverage was brown and hot and nothing a handful of sugar packets and some cream couldn't manage to make drinkable.

Pain laid out the best spread he could carry with two hands

and, for not the first time in recent memory, said, "Canada sounds better and better to me lately."

"And why is that?" Agony doctored her coffee and bit into a muffin.

"Because other than the old couple who were my hosts in 2001 who have no doubt passed away by now, no one there knows me. It would be the perfect opposite of the *Cheers* bar where everyone knows your name. Tell me it's not a tempting proposition."

"Let me make this perfectly clear. If I have to relocate to a place where no one knows my name, it had better damn well have sandy beaches twelve months out of any given year and where you would have to climb to the top of a mountain if you wanted to find any snow."

"Okay. Nix on Canada, except for maybe a short visit in the month of August."

"I'm glad we got that out of the way. The muffins are not as fresh as advertised but the eggs are acceptable."

"The bacon is a little undercooked for my taste."

Agony thought the bacon was juicy and perfectly done. "Don't tell me. You are a burnt-bacon kind of guy?"

Pain nodded as he spread something that resembled butter on a slice of toast. "The crispier the better. I prefer all my pork products to be just this side of charred."

"Speaking of charred. Special Agent Marshal Buchanan?"

"We did what we had to do. To quote Forrest Gump, 'That's all I have to say about that.'"

"Fair enough." She sighed and sipped her coffee. "Now what? We can't keep bouncing from hotel to hotel. I would like to be able to unpack and settle in for a while."

"Ahjoomenoni?" He raised an eyebrow when she didn't answer immediately.

"I miss the food at Kwan's," she said finally. "Do you think she's rented our apartments to other tenants already?"

Pain made a face and shook his head, although she wasn't sure if that was a response to her question or a critique of the coffee. "That's not her style."

"And why would that be?"

"She hasn't survived this long by doing anything in haste unless pushed. We didn't push her. She pushed us. That is one of the ways you learn how to earn her trust. Her only concern was Buchanan, not Morris the powerful but pesky perv. For better or worse, we have relieved her of her FBI worries. She merely doesn't know it yet."

Agony grimaced as she tried another bite of a muffin before she gave up all hope on its freshness and tossed it on her plate. "Then I guess we need to check in and try to get back in her good graces?"

"Something like that, yeah," he agreed. "But we will go there to report, not to grovel. We still haven't dug into Eddie the Getty's stash and I would rather not. What we want—no, need—is to stay on her good side."

She snorted. "I remember the good old days when my only question for my landlord was whether they could send up some heat instead of AC in November. But what do we have to prove to her that Buchanan is now out of the equation?"

Pain pulled a badge out of one of his pockets and placed it on the table.

"As I carried him to the furnace chute, I may have relieved him of this. We would need it more than he would. I feel a little guilty for having pick-pocketed a dead man but I'll get over it."

Agony looked down and picked up Special Agent Marshal Buchanan's FBI badge to have a closer look.

"This expires next year so it is due for renewal soon."

He agreed. "Which means it is still valid. Our sweet little old landlady knows that a fed like Buchanan would never surrender his badge. That should be proof enough."

She placed the badge gently on the table. "We have two

hours before we have to check out. Not knowing if we will have a place to sleep tonight, I would dearly love to have a shower and a fresh set of clothes to wear when we confront her."

"I'm on it."

Pain headed out and down to Bertha where he retrieved a couple of suitcases and hauled them up to their room.

"Are you checking in?" the clerk at the front door asked as he carried the luggage through the small lobby.

He shook his head and gave the clerk a tired smile. "No. We're checking out soon but she forgot her cosmetic cases."

The man glanced at the two pieces of luggage and showed every sign of understanding. "Would you like me to put you down for a late check-out?"

"Room two-twenty-four." He smiled his appreciation. "Twelve noon as opposed to eleven would be very much appreciated."

"Noon it is." The clerk returned the smile.

Pain lugged the luggage to the elevator and stepped inside when the door opened.

The clerk updated the check-out time for room two-twenty-four and made sure that the elevator door had closed before he muttered, "Poor bastard."

The partners showered and changed into fresh clothes and beat the noon check-out time by ten minutes.

The clerk saw the big man give him another smile while he carried the two large suitcases to the lobby's exit. He also saw a striking-looking woman at his side, who also smiled.

She didn't look like she had even a drop of make-up on her face, and he changed his opinion from poor to lucky bastard.

Pain loaded the suitcases into Bertha and took the wheel as Agony slid into the passenger seat. Before he pulled out and not knowing what else they would encounter before the day was done, he had one more question on his mind.

"How's the arm?"

She closed her eyes and leaned back against the headrest. "I think we might need to go back and visit Iggy again."

"Iggy or Miles? Does it hurt that much? Do you need stronger pain killers?"

She kept her eyes closed as she answered. "Iggy. Definitely Iggy."

"Shit. Do you think he missed something?"

"He missed putting a hard-cast on my forearm so I could use it to crack your head open if you ask me about my arm again." She sounded very serious.

"Oh. One time too many?" He decided not to apologize for caring.

"Something like that, yeah." Having said her piece, she straightened. "I do think, though, that I would like to swing past whatever is left of our office to see if it's been ransacked before we meet our landlady."

"Fair enough."

Pain changed their route and found a space on the Pasha's Deli side of the stairs leading to their office. They took a moment to pause and breathe the aromas in. Nothing from a chain hotel's kitchen could match it. Sighing, they headed up the stairs.

The open space where the etched window of their office door used to be still had crime-scene tape crisscrossing it. A second layer of tape had also been applied to the lower half of the entrance. One would have to be a fourth-level contortionist to have been able to get past it.

Satisfied that whatever had been inside when they had been raided would still be there when they returned, they headed down the stairs. They had a landlady to deal with.

A short while later, the partners pulled into the parking lot that was Bertha's home.

Game Show George welcomed them with a smile as he raised the bar to give them access.

"I got a call-back for *High or Low?*" he shouted as they paused before they entered the lot. "And it's filmed right here in the city. All I got to do is act like a fool and guess how much something costs in Paris, France. Or how much the same thing would cost in Kansas City, Missouri. And here's the secret—you don't wanna win the prize of cruises or all expenses paid vacations. There are all kinds of hidden taxes and fees you gotta pay, not to mention the time you have to take off from work to enjoy those. No, sirree! What those in the know say is that you want to come in second. That way, you get paid a grand for one day's worth of work. How sweet is that?"

"Very sweet, George. Good luck. We have to give Bertha a rest now."

"Righty-oh! How is the old girl? You took her on a road trip, did'ja?"

Pain laughed. "Something like that."

George used his best game show announcer's voice. "Then come on in!"

He did exactly that and parked. They exited Bertha but left all their earthy belongings locked securely in the back and waved at George as they crossed the parking lot toward Kwan's.

"One grand," the guard called, "just to spend a day coming in second!"

"Sweet deal! Happy losing!" he called in response.

"You'll never be a loser in my book, George!" Agony hollered at him.

Game Show George spent the rest of his shift with a smile on his face. They were a strange couple but his favorites.

The partners walked toward Kwan's and Agony admitted, "My arm still is a little sore."

"Then please allow me to be hauled in first."

Pain didn't wait for either a response from his partner or for anyone to haul them in. He marched straight through Kwan's door without an invitation and walked calmly through the late-lunch crowd to the private back dining room where he knew Ahjoomenoni would be conducting her real business. His partner followed in silence.

Once in the back room, there was a quick scuffle and they stood in front of the table where Ahjoomenoni studied her paperwork. Three of her personal bodyguards had been relieved of their weapons and were left seated on the floor off to the side, most of the damage having been done to their egos.

Their landlady didn't even look up from her papers. "What took you so long?"

Pain bowed slightly. "I would have been able to speak ten seconds earlier if you would please not have someone try to put a gun to the side of my head every time I come to give you a progress report."

"That is a very reasonable request. I shall take it under consideration." Ahjoomenoni looked up. "Do you have something you wish to report?"

Pain placed Special Agent Marshal Buchanan's FBI ID on her table and stepped back to give her time to inspect it. She didn't need a magnifying glass to confirm its validity.

"Agent Buchanan?"

"Will never darken your doorstep again. He was after someone else and used you as a smokescreen."

Ahjoomenoni understood. "Yes, I am very useful to many as a —what you say, smokescreen?"

He gave another slight bow. "Surely that comes as no surprise."

"Very little surprises me these days, Gotong. And you, Ms. Alicia Goni. What surprises you?"

Agony had learned enough to know when to give a slight bow before responding. "I am always surprised to learn that respect can be earned and returned. Trust is a very rare commodity these days."

The woman smiled at her. "Trust has always been a rare commodity."

Pain was tired of being homeless and officeless as he and his partner had been after all their belongings had been dumped in the back alley. Given all they had been through, he took a chance and interrupted.

He didn't even bother to bow. "With your permission, Ahjoomenoni, I will now go up to my apartment. And tomorrow, I will return to my office and resume working."

Ahjoomenoni glanced at Agony.

"I'm with the band."

The partners then had the audacity to turn their backs on her and marched out through the main dining room and up the stairs to their apartments. Their landlady allowed herself a slight smile as she watched them go, then put her frown-face on again as her security force returned to consciousness.

"Will you boys please not allow any further interruptions? I have paperwork that needs to be done."

The boys scrambled to their feet and took their on-guard stations. Any questions they had could be asked between themselves at a later time.

In silence, the partners trudged up the stairs. Their belongings in Bertha could wait until tomorrow to be brought up. When they reached the top of the stairs, Pain pulled his key out and was relieved to learn that his apartment door's lock had not been changed.

Agony felt the same relief when she opened her door. She turned to face her partner and was not smiling. "My apartment? My office?"

"What else was I supposed to say?" he asked.

"You could have said *our* apartments, and *our* office—that is the way partners talk."

Properly chastised, he could only respond with, "It's been a long time since I've had a partner. I'm still getting used to the lingo."

"You and me both."

"Mañana?"

She sighed. "Sure. Unless I find a better partner tonight, then mañana it is. But you had better have one helluva pot of coffee waiting for me."

THE STORY CONTINUES

The story continues with book 4, *The Fires of Hell*, coming soon to Amazon and to Kindle Unlimited.

Claim your copy today!

CREATOR NOTES
NOVEMBER 1, 2021

Thank you for not only reading this story but these author notes as well.

I'm in Sharjah, UAE at the moment for the 2021 Sharjah Book Fair. I'm on a panel about whether science fiction helps direct humanity's efforts in the far future.

It's presently 4:47 AM here (about 5:57 PM back in Las Vegas). I feel like I'm never going to get a full night's sleep ever again in my life.

Jet lag sucks.

(*Editor's note: totally agree. I got up at 4am this morning after falling asleep at 8pm. Usually I don't start working until 8 or 9pm and I go to bed about 4am.*)

Ok, that's enough about my wicked time schedule. Let's talk about kicking ass and taking NO names!

So, I dreamt up Pain & Agony as a pair of bombastic (Ha! See what I did there?) characters who are tossed together one fateful night. Now we see them together in all sorts of situations where regardless of their annoyance with each other, they DO care about the other.

Kind of. Well, they grow on each other. Perhaps Agony

believes Pain grows on her like lichen, but hey, it's still growth. Right?

Right?

I think I'll just let that one lie right there.

On another note, I have read many of the reviews, and I have to admit I get a kick out of the ones that discuss Alicia and M's names. Sometimes I believe I'm clever when I am just famished and need carbs or protein and my brain isn't thinking straight.

So, for those of you who mentioned the Pain and Agony's names in your reviews, know I have read all, and I am accepting your enjoyment of the names as silent approval from most of the readers on the names.

Probably because my author's fragile ego couldn't handle the truth. LOL.

Ok, it's time I wrapped up these author notes. Hope I didn't say anything too stupid above, and if I did, Lynne PLEASE edit it out.

(*Editor's note: I got your back, big guy!*)

Have a great week or weekend, and talk to you in the next book!

Ad Aeternitatem,
Michael Anderle

BOOKS BY MICHAEL ANDERLE

Sign up for the LMBPN email list to be notified of new releases and special deals!

https://lmbpn.com/email/

For a complete list of books by Michael Anderle, please visit:

www.lmbpn.com/ma-books/

CONNECT WITH MICHAEL

Connect with Michael Anderle

Website: http://lmbpn.com

Email List: http://lmbpn.com/email/

https://www.facebook.com/LMBPNPublishing

https://twitter.com/MichaelAnderle

https://www.instagram.com/lmbpn_publishing/

https://www.bookbub.com/authors/michael-anderle

Made in the USA
Monee, IL
01 April 2022